一盅诗酒债

许渊冲译唐诗三百首

许渊冲 译

300 Tang Poems Classified by Time

汉英双语朗读版

朗读者：李玲玲 李 响

商務印書館国际有限公司
中国·北京

图书在版编目（CIP）数据

一盅诗酒债 ：许渊冲译唐诗三百首 ：汉英对照 / 许渊冲译 . -- 北京 ：商务印书馆国际有限公司，2022.10
ISBN 978-7-5176-0946-9

I. ①一… II. ①许… III. ①唐诗－诗集－汉、英 IV. ① I222.742

中国版本图书馆 CIP 数据核字（2022）第 170482 号

300 Tang Poems Classified by Time
一盅诗酒债——许渊冲译唐诗三百首

译　者	许渊冲
出版发行	商务印书馆国际有限公司
地　址	北京市朝阳区吉庆里 14 号楼佳汇国际中心 A 座 12 层
邮　编	100020
电　话	010-65592876（编校部） 010-65598498（市场营销部）
网　址	www.cpi1993.com
印　刷	大地飞达（天津）印刷有限公司
开　本	787mm×1092mm 1/32
字　数	700 千字
印　张	23.25
版　次	2022 年 10 月第 1 版第 1 次印刷
书　号	ISBN 978-7-5176-0946-9
定　价	98.00 元

出版前言

本书即将付梓，许渊冲先生却已溘然长逝一年有余。回忆先生的音容笑貌历历如在眼前，我们每次去先生家里拜访，他都会滔滔不绝地介绍自己最新的翻译成果，拿出最新出版的图书评论其优长。看着年届百岁的先生依然如此孜孜不倦、如此乐此不疲地投身翻译工作，作为后生晚辈，在崇敬之余，每个人内心都会油然升起时不我待的紧迫感。

先生在接受采访时曾说过“生命并不是你活了多少日子，而是你记住了多少日子”。在先生 100 年的生命长河中，他用勤奋的工作记录了每一个日子，让生命的质和量都达到了常人难以企及的高度。先生是西南联大的高材生，致力于英语教学和翻译八十余年，专精中英、中法互译，共有译著 100 余部，他将很大一部分精力投入中国优秀传统文化精粹的翻译，很早以前，就有唐诗宋词等方面的译著由海外知名出版机构出版，同时为中国人带来了精妙绝伦的英法文学作品。先生在耄耋之年，仍然给自己制定了“每天翻译1000字”的工作计划，93岁时为自己制定了翻译莎士比亚全集的目标。先生被誉为“诗译英法唯一人”，曾获“中国翻译文化终身成就奖”和国际翻译界最高奖项之一的“北极光”杰出文学翻译奖等殊荣。

《唐诗三百首》是许渊冲先生的代表译作之一。唐代是中国历史上最辉煌、最强盛的时期之一，诗歌在这一时期达到了她的又一个巅峰。为能更好地概说那个时代的诗歌特点，本书书名最终确定为《一盅诗酒债——许渊冲译唐诗三百首》。著名书法家徐康岩先生题写了书名，书中部分插画由以师承宋元山水见长的著名画家何松提供。本书一方面是给喜欢英文翻译的爱好者提供一个学习的参照，另一方面也让国外的读者了解中国诗歌的韵律美、意境美。

为了出好先生的译作，做到文质兼美，拿到先生的授权之后，出版团队心存敬畏，精心设计版式，认真核改清样，反复推敲、设计封面和书名，邀请专业的中英文播音员朗读古诗词和先生的译作，并配以古琴音乐作为背景，尽最大努力将经典诗词与先生精妙的译作的美呈现给亲爱的读者。

我们怀着敬意和忐忑将这部作品敬献给先生的在天之灵，也希望我们的努力能得到广大读者的认可。

目　录

一、花舞大唐春

二、饮酣视八极，俗物都茫茫

三、留得枯荷听雨声

一

花舞大唐春

·初唐·

代表一个时代的，往往不是那个时代盛行一时的。正如以绮错婉媚风行初唐的上官体无法代表初唐诗风一样。真正的初唐诗，甫一出世，便冲破了东晋玄言，洗尽了六朝铅华，上接无邪诗韵，中续建安风骨，自成一格。它虽然略显粗砺横蛮，但却具有了雄劲无俦的开创性——唐诗，从初唐开始更多了种狂飙突进的气势，睥睨天下的自信。这种气势与自信即使在安史之乱的烽火笼罩下，在晚唐牧笛的呜咽中也未曾断绝，时露峥嵘；正是这种气势与自信，使我们每每梦回过去所看到的大唐天空，总是那么生气勃勃、阳刚浩然；正是这种气势与自信，塑造了初唐的气质，开辟了初唐的诗风——慷慨兴寄，骨气充沛。

春江花月夜

张若虚

春江潮水连海平，
海上明月共潮生。
滟滟随波千万里，
何处春江无月明。
江流宛转绕芳甸，
月照花林皆似霰。
空里流霜不觉飞，
汀上白沙看不见。
江天一色无纤尘，
皎皎空中孤月轮。
江畔何人初见月？
江月何年初照人？

The Moon over the River on a Spring Night

Zhang Ruoxu

In spring the river rises as high as the sea,
And with the river's tide uprises the moon bright.
She follows the rolling waves for ten thousand *li*;
Where'er the river flows, there overflows her light.
The river winds around the fragrant islet where
The blooming flowers in her light all look like snow.
You cannot tell her beams from hoar frost in the air,
Nor from white sand upon the Farewell Beach below.
No dust has stained the water blending with the skies;
A lonely wheel-like moon shines brilliant far and wide.
Who by the riverside did first see the moon rise?
When did the moon first see a man by riverside?

人生代代无穷已，
江月年年只相似。
不知江月待何人，
但见长江送流水。
白云一片去悠悠，
青枫浦上不胜愁。
谁家今夜扁舟子？
何处相思明月楼？
可怜楼上月徘徊，
应照离人妆镜台。
玉户帘中卷不去，
捣衣砧上拂还来。
此时相望不相闻，
愿逐月华流照君。
鸿雁长飞光不度，
鱼龙潜跃水成文。
昨夜闲潭梦落花，

Many generations have come and passed away;
From year to year the moons look alike, old and new.
We do not know tonight for whom she sheds her ray,
But hear the river say to its water adieu.
Away, away is sailing a single cloud white;
On Farewell Beach are pining away maples green.
Where is the wanderer sailing his boat tonight?
Who, pining away, on the moonlit rails would lean?
Alas! The moon is lingering over the tower;
It should have seen her dressing table all alone.
She may roll curtains up, but light is in her bower;
She may wash, but moonbeams still remain on the stone.
She sees the moon, but her husband is out of sight;
She would follow the moonbeams to shine on his face.
But message-bearing swans can't fly out of moonlight,
Nor letter-sending fish can leap out of their place.
He dreamed of flowers falling o'er the pool last night;

可怜春半不还家。
江水流春去欲尽，
江潭落月复西斜。
斜月沉沉藏海雾，
碣石潇湘无限路。
不知乘月几人归，
落月摇情满江树。

Alas! Spring has half gone, but he can't homeward go.

The water bearing spring will run away in flight;

The moon over the pool will in the west sink low.

In the mist on the sea the slanting moon will hide;

It's a long way from northern hills to southern streams.

How many can go home by moonlight on the tide?

The setting moon sheds o'er riverside trees but dreams.

* *This poem describes five of the most beautiful things in nature: spring, river, flowers, moon, night. The poet writes about a beautiful woman among flowers under the moon on a spring night, thinking of her love sailing on the river. Thus the beauty of nature mingles with the love of man.*

于易水送人一绝

骆宾王

此地别燕丹，
壮士发冲冠。
昔时人已没，
今日水犹寒。

Farewell on River Yi

Luo Binwang

The hero left his friend

With angry hair on end.

The martyr's now no more,

The waves cold as of yore.

* *The hero and martyr refers to Jing Ke who left his friends on River Yi and planned to kill the king of Qin but failed.*

咏 蝉

骆宾王

西陆蝉声唱，
南冠客思深。
那堪玄鬓影，
来对白头吟。
露重飞难进，
风多响易沉。
无人信高洁，
谁为表予心。

The Cicada

Luo Binwang

Of autumn the cicada sings;
In prison I'm worn out with care.
How can I bear its blue black wings,
Which remind me of my grey hair?
Heavy with dew it cannot fly;
Drowned in the wind, its song's not heard.
Who would believe its spirit high?
Could I express my grief in word?

* *Hearing in prison the cicada sing, the poet compares himself to a cicada which cannot fly and whose song cannot be heard.*

登幽州台歌

陈子昂

前不见古人，
后不见来者。
念天地之悠悠，
独怆然而涕下。

On the Tower at Youzhou

Chen Zi'ang

Where are the great men of the past
And where are those of future years?
The sky and earth forever last;
Here and now I alone shed tears.

* *The poet sighs for he has not done great deeds as the great men of yore.*

感遇

陈子昂

兰若生春夏，
芊蔚何青青！
幽独空林色，
朱蕤冒紫茎。
迟迟白日晚，
嫋嫋秋风生。
岁华尽摇落，
芳意竟何成？

The Orchid

Chen Zi'ang

In late spring grows the orchid good,
How luxuriant are its leaves green!
Alone it adorns empty wood
With red blooms and violet stems lean.
Slowly, slowly shortens the day;
Rippling, rippling blows autumn breeze.
By the year's end it fades away.
What has become of it fragrance, please?

* *The poet compares himself to the fragrant orchid which grows in late spring in an empty wood and fades away by the year's end.*

山　中

王　勃

长江悲已滞，
万里念将归。
况属高风晚，
山山黄叶飞。

In the Mountains

Wang Bo

The Long River grieves over my long stay,

For my home is a thousand miles away.

Now blows the evening wind so high;

From mountain to mountain yellow leaves fly.

* *The poet staying in the mountains thinks of his home far away when autumn leaves fall.*

咏风

王勃

肃肃凉风生，
加我林壑清。
驱烟寻涧户，
卷雾出山楹。
去来固无迹，
动息如有情。
日落山水静，
为君起松声。

The Breeze

Wang Bo

Soughing, the cool breeze blows;
My wooded dell clean grows.
It drives smoke off the rill,
Rolls up mist over the hill,
Leaves no trace when we part,
And moves as if moved at heart.
When sunset calms the scene,
Hear the song of pines green.

* *The poet praises the breeze which appeals to our eyes by cleaning the dell and to our ears by making the pines sing their green song.*

送杜少府之任蜀川

王　勃

城阙辅三秦，
风烟望五津。
与君离别意，
同是宦游人。
海内存知己，
天涯若比邻。
无为在歧路，
儿女共沾巾。

Farewell to Prefect Du

Wang Bo

You'll leave the town walled far and wide
For mist-veiled land by riverside.
I feel on parting sad and drear
For both of us are strangers here.
If you have friends who know your heart,
Distance cannot keep you apart.
At crossroads where we bid adieu,
Do not shed tears as women do!

* *The poet consoles his friend by saying that distance cannot keep bosom friends apart.*

渡汉江

宋之问

岭外音书断，
经冬复历春。
近乡情更怯，
不敢问来人。

Crossing River Han

Song Zhiwen

I longed for news on the frontier
From day to day, from year to year.
Now nearing home, timid I grow,
I dare not ask what I would know.

* *This quatrain describes the contradictory mind of the banished poet.*

题大庾岭北驿

宋之问

阳月南飞雁，
传闻至此回。
我行殊未已，
何日复归来？
江静潮初落，
林昏瘴不开。
明朝望乡处，
应见陇头梅。

At the Northern Post of the Peak of Mumes

Song Zhiwen

In the tenth moon wild geese south fly;
They will turn back at this peak high.
But I must farther southward go.
When may I come back? Do you know?
The river's calm when ebbs the tide;
Dense fog darkens the forest wide.
Tomorrow looking for my homeland,
I can only see mume trees stand.

* *It was believed that the south-going wild geese would not pass the Peak of Mumes. The banished poet thinks he is not so fortunate as the wild geese for he must go farther south.*

送别杜审言

宋之问

卧病人事绝，
嗟君万里行。
河桥不相送，
江树远含情。
别路追孙楚，
维舟吊屈平。
可惜龙泉剑，
流落在丰城。

Farewell to Du Shenyan (Grandfather of Du Fu)

Song Zhiwen

Ill, visited by none each day,

I sigh for you'll go far away.

I cannot bid farewell to you.

Let riverside tree say adieu!

A hero may not serve till old;

A poet's drowned in river cold.

The precious sword of Dragon's Fountain

Might still shine bright though in deep mountain.

* *The "poet" here refers to Qu Yuan who drowned himself in River Miluo in 278 BC.*

从军行

杨　炯

烽火照西京，
心中自不平。
牙璋辞凤阙，
铁骑绕龙城。
雪暗凋旗画，
风多杂鼓声。
宁为百夫长，
胜作一书生。

I Would Rather Fight

Yang Jiong

The beacon fires spread to the capital;

My agitated mind can't be calmed down.

By royal order to leave palace hall;

Our armored steeds besiege the Dragon Town.

Darkening snow damages our banners red;

With the howling wind mingle our drumbeats.

I'd rather fight at a hundred men's head

Than pore over books without performing feats.

* *The poet would rather fight than write.*

代悲白头翁

刘希夷

洛阳城东桃李花，
飞来飞去落谁家？
洛阳女儿惜颜色，
坐见落花长叹息。
今年花落颜色改，
明年花开复谁在？
已见松柏摧为薪，
更闻桑田变成海。
古人无复洛城东，
今人还对落花风。
年年岁岁花相似，

Admonition on the Part of a White-haired Old Man

Liu Xiyi

The peach and plum flowers east of the capital
Fly up and down and here and there. Where will they fall?
The maiden in the capital loves rosy hue;
She would sigh for the flowers falling out of view.
Her rosy color fades when flowers fall this year.
When flowers blow again, will she pretty appear?
I've seen cypress cut down as fuel with pine trees;
I've heard the mulberry fields turn into the seas.
We see no ancients now east of capital town,
But we still see today the wind blow flowers down.
The flowers of this year look like those of last year;

岁岁年年人不同。
寄言全盛红颜子，
应怜半死白头翁。
此翁白头真可怜，
伊昔红颜美少年。
公子王孙芳树下，
清歌妙舞落花前。
光禄池台文锦绣，
将军楼阁画神仙。
一朝卧病无相识，
三春行乐在谁边？
婉转蛾眉能几时？
须臾鹤发乱如丝。
但看古来歌舞地，
唯有黄昏鸟雀悲！

But next year the same people will not reappear.
I'd like to tell the rosy faces in their prime
Not to forget the old before their dying time.
Pitiable is the old man whose hair turns white,
But in his prime he was rosy-cheeked, fair and bright.
Noble sons and daughters under the leafy trees
Sing and dance before the flowers blown down by the breeze.
By lakeside stand ministers' richly brocaded bowers;
Pictures of immortals hang in generals' towers.
When you're ill and cast down, with you none would abide.
Who would then make merry in spring days by your side?
How long can your finely arched eyebrows remain fair?
Your head will soon be covered with disheveled hair.
See where the noble sang and danced in merriment,
Now you can only hear at dusk the birds' lament.

* *The poet admonishes young men and maidens not to waste their golden hours of youth.*

二

饮酣视八极
俗物都茫茫

·盛唐·

汉唐雄风，大国气象，铺展在诗行里，便呈现出鲸吸百川、千帆竞发的景象。从建安七子应可窥魏晋风流的全豹；以初唐四杰代表初唐诗坛也算是差强人意；婉约豪放四字大体上也能把宋词说个七七八八……但我们却无法用几句话就概括了盛唐的诗，更无法用李杜、王孟代表盛唐的诗坛——那是一场空前绝后的海天盛筵——异彩纷呈，包罗万象。李白的绣口吐不尽半个盛唐；杜甫的沉郁遮不住江南烟雨；高岑的边塞朔风吹不去坝上柳絮；王孟的山水田畴也阻隔不了长安街市的繁华与喧嚣……盛唐的诗风变动不居、鬼神难测，它具备了所有风的形态，值得无数次涵泳优游——吹拂万物，流转不歇——诗，到了盛唐才真正拥有了他的魂魄、他的气象。

春　晓

孟浩然

春眠不觉晓，
处处闻啼鸟。
夜来风雨声，
花落知多少。

A Spring Morning

Meng Haoran

This spring morning in bed I'm lying,
Not to awake till birds are crying.
After one night of wind and showers,
How many are the fallen flowers!

* *This quatrain reveals the poet's love of spring and his regret of her departure.*

晚泊浔阳望庐山

孟浩然

挂席几千里，
名山都未逢。
泊舟浔阳郭，
始见香炉峰。
尝读远公传，
永怀尘外踪。
东林精舍近，
日暮但闻钟。

Mount Lu Viewed from Xunyang at Dusk

Meng Haoran

For miles and miles I sail and float;
High-famed mountains are hard to seek.
By riverside I moor my boat,
Then I perceive the Censer Peak.
Knowing the hermit's life and way,
I love his solitary dell.
His hermitage not far away,
I hear at sunset but the bell.

* *Mount Lu is a high-famed mountain with one of its peaks looking like a censer. The poet gazes on it at dusk from Xunyang, present-day Jiujiang, a town by the riverside, and speaks of his admiration of the hermit who lived in the East Forest Temple at the foot of the mountain hundreds of years ago. The bell rings from the temple makes the poet feel the tranquillity of the hermit's life.*

留别王维

孟浩然

寂寂竟何待，
朝朝空自归。
欲寻芳草去，
惜与故人违。
当路谁相假，
知音世所稀。
只应守寂寞，
还掩故园扉。

Parting from Wang Wei

Meng Haoran

Lonely, lonely, what is there to hope for?

Day by day I come back without an end.

I would seek fragrant grass in native shore.

How I regret to part with my old friend!

I'm one whom those in high place would elude,

For there are few connoisseurs in the state.

I can but keep myself in solitude

And go back to close my old garden gate.

* *The poet will leave the capital after his failure in the civil service examinations.*

送杜十四之江南

孟浩然

荆吴相接水为乡，
君去春江正渺茫。
日暮征帆何处泊？
天涯一望断人肠。

Seeing Du Fourteenth off to the East

Meng Haoran

The east and west are joined by boundless water clear;

On the endless spring river goes the boat you steer.

Where will you moor it at sunset far, far apart?

Can I not gaze far, far away with broken heart!

* *The poet speaks of his longing for his friend at parting.*

送魏万之京

李　颀

朝闻游子唱离歌，
昨夜微霜初渡河。
鸿雁不堪愁里听，
云山况是客中过。
关城树色催寒近，
御苑砧声向晚多。
莫见长安行乐处，
空令岁月易蹉跎。

Seeing Wei Wan off to the Capital

Li Qi

At dawn I hear the roamer's farewell song;
Last night a thin frost crossed the river long.
Are you not grieved to hear the wild geese cry?
Can you bear clouds and mountains passing by?
Yellow leaves hasten the cold to come near.
Could washerwomen's song reach their men's ear?
Don't make merry in the capital town
And waste the prime of your life up and down!

* *The poet advises his friend to think more of the hardship than of the pleasure in the capital.*

送刘昱

李　颀

八月寒苇花，
秋江浪头白。
北风吹五两，
谁是浔阳客。
鸬鹚山头微雨晴，
扬州郭里暮潮生。
行人夜宿金陵渚，
试听沙边有雁声。

Farewell to Liu Yu

Li Qi

In the eighth moon the weed cold grows,

The autumn waves surge with white crest.

The mast shivers as north wind blows;

Why should my guest go to the west?

The rain no longer drizzles on hilltop;

Out of the door rises the evening tide.

At night along the beach my friend should stop.

Hear lonely wild goose cry by riverside!

* *This is a dreary picture of parting in autumn.*

古从军行

李　颀

白日登山望烽火，
黄昏饮马傍交河。
行人刁斗风沙暗，
公主琵琶幽怨多。
野营万里无城郭，
雨雪纷纷连大漠。
胡雁哀鸣夜夜飞，
胡儿眼泪双双落。
闻道玉门犹被遮，
应将性命逐轻车。
年年战骨埋荒外，
空见蒲桃入汉家。

Army Life

Li Qi

We climb up mountains to watch for beacon fires,
And water horses by riverside when day expires.
We beat the gong in sand-darkened land where wind blows,
And hear the pipa tell the princess' secret woe.
There is no town for miles and miles but tents in rows;
Beyond the desert there's nothing but rain and snow.
The wild geese honk from night to night, that's all we hear;
We see but Tartar soldiers shedding tear on tear.
'Tis said we cannot go back through the Jade Gate Pass;
We'd risk our lives to follow war-chariots, alas!
The dead are buried in the desert year by year,
Only to bring back grapes from over the frontier.

* *The poet draws a desolate picture of the army life on the frontier.*

送陈章甫

李　颀

四月南风大麦黄，
枣花未落桐叶长。
青山朝别暮还见，
嘶马出门思旧乡。
陈侯立身何坦荡，
虬须虎眉仍大颡。
腹中贮书一万卷，
不肯低头在草莽。
东门酤酒饮我曹，
心轻万事如鸿毛。
醉卧不知白日暮，

Farewell to Chen Zhangfu

Li Qi

To yellow barley the summer wind sings its song,
Date flowers not yet fallen, the plain leaves grow long.
Green hills left at dawn can be seen at dusk again;
The horse neighing outdoors thinks of its familiar plain.
My friend, you are so dignified and frank and true.
With dragon beard, tiger brows and large forehead too,
In your bosom there must be ten thousand books you've read;
To the officialdom you would not bow your head.
By the east gate you drink wine with us in delight;
At heart you take everything as a feather light.
Without knowing the sun has set, so drunk you lie;

有时空望孤云高。
长河浪头连天黑，
津吏停舟渡不得。
郑国游人未及家，
洛阳行子空叹息！
闻道故林相识多，
罢官昨日今如何。

Sometimes you gaze in vain at lonely cloud on high.
Waves in the long river surge to join the dark sky;
No boat at the ferry would take the passers-by.
Roamer, you cannot go back to your native land,
Sighing in vain by the riverside where you stand.
You have many friends in your country, people say,
Dismissed yesterday, how will they greet you today?

* *The poet bids farewell at the ferry to a friend dismissed from his office.*

送魏二

王昌龄

醉别江楼橘柚香，
江风引雨入舟凉。
忆君遥在潇湘月，
愁听清猿梦里长。

Farewell to Wei the Second

Wang Changling

Drunk, we leave the wine shop sweetened with orange blooms;

The breeze brings in your boat the rain casting cold glooms.

When steeped in moonlight far away in Southern streams,

You would be grieved to hear monkeys' wail in your dreams.

* *This quatrain is written when the poet is banished from the capital.*

芙蓉楼送辛渐

王昌龄

寒雨连江夜入吴，
平明送客楚山孤。
洛阳亲友如相问，
一片冰心在玉壶。

Farewell to Xin Jian at Lotus Tower

Wang Changling

A cold rain dissolved in East Stream invades the night;
At dawn you'll leave the lonely Southern hills in haze.
If my friends in the North should ask if I'm all right,
Tell them I'm free from blame as ice in crystal vase.

* *The poet speaks of his innocence at parting with his friend.*

出　塞

王昌龄

秦时明月汉时关，
万里长征人未还。
但使龙城飞将在，
不教胡马度阴山。

On the Frontier

Wang Changling

The moon still shines on mountain passes as of yore.

How many guardsmen of the Great Wall are no more!

If the Flying General were still there in command,

No hostile steeds would have dared to invade our land.

* *The poet sympathizes with the guardsmen and glorifies General Li who defeated the foe.*

从军行（其四）

王昌龄

青海长云暗雪山，
孤城遥望玉门关。
黄沙百战穿金甲，
不破楼兰终不还。

Poems on Army Life (IV)

Wang Changling

Clouds on frontier overshadow mountains clad in snow;

A lonely town afar faces Pass of Jade Gate.

Our golden armor pierced by sand, we fight the foe;

We won't come back till we destroy the hostile State.

* *This quatrain shows the fighting spirit of the army.*

从军行（其五）

王昌龄

大漠风尘日色昏，
红旗半卷出辕门。
前军夜战洮河北，
已报生擒吐谷浑。

Poems on Army Life (V)

Wang Changling

The wind and sand in the desert have dimmed sunlight;

With red flags half unfurled we go through the camp gate.

North of River Tao, after nocturnal fight,

Our vanguards have captured the chief of hostile State.

* *The poet describes the victory won by the army after one battle at night.*

终南望余雪

祖　咏

终南阴岭秀，
积雪浮云端。
林表明霁色，
城中增暮寒。

Snow atop the Southern Mountains

Zu Yong

How fair the gloomy mountainside!

Snow-crowned peaks float above the cloud.

The forest's bright in sunset dyed,

With evening cold the town's overflowed.

* *This poem is well-known for its description of natural beauties: the snow-crowned peaks mingling with floating cloud, and the gloomy forest on the mountainside brightened as if dyed by the setting sun.*

望蓟门

祖　咏

燕台一望客心惊，
笳鼓喧喧汉将营。
万里寒光生积雪，
三边曙色动危旌。
沙场烽火连胡月，
海畔云山拥蓟城。
少小虽非投笔吏，
论功还欲请长缨。

Gazing on Northern Gate

Zu Yong

My mind is startled when I've left the Northern town,
To hear horns and drums in General's camp up and down.
For miles and miles cold light grows out of piled-up snow;
In twilight on frontier flags flutter high and low.
The beacon fire brightens the moon on battleground
And clouds over the seaside town, mountains surround.
While young, I did not give up the pen for the sword;
To do a feat, I would capture the Tartar lord.

* *Gazing on the Northern frontier, the poet wishes to do a feat.*

辛夷坞

王　维

木末芙蓉花，
山中发红萼。
涧户寂无人，
纷纷开且落。

The Magnolia Dale

Wang Wei

The magnolia-tipped trees

In mountains burst in flowers.

The mute brook-side house sees

Them blow and fall in showers.

* *This quatrain reveals the poet's sympathy with the magnolia flowers which burst in blossom and then fall on decline.*

竹里馆

王　维

独坐幽篁里，
弹琴复长啸。
深林人不知，
明月来相照。

The Bamboo Hut

Wang Wei

Sitting among bamboos alone,

I play on lute and croon carefree.

In the deep woods where I'm unknown,

Only the bright moon peeps at me.

* *This quatrain describes the communion of a solitary lutist with nature, that is, the solitary moon and a solitary bamboo grove.*

山　中

王　维

荆溪白石出，
天寒红叶稀。
山路元无雨，
空翠湿人衣。

In the Hills

Wang Wei

White pebbles hear a blue stream glide;

Red leaves are strewn on cold hillside.

Along the path no rain is seen,

My gown is moist with drizzling green.

* *This is a colorful picture of the hills: white pebbles, blue stream, red leaves and the drizzling green which can not only be seen but also heard and felt.*

相　思

王　维

红豆生南国，
春来发几枝？
愿君多采撷，
此物最相思。

Love Seeds

Wang Wei

The red beans grow in southern land.

How many load in spring the trees?

Gather them till full in your hand;

They would revive fond memories.

* *The red beans are called love seeds.*

杂诗（其二）

王 维

君自故乡来，
应知故乡事。
来日绮窗前，
寒梅著花未。

Our Native Place

Wang Wei

You come from native place,

What happened there you'd know.

Did mume blossoms in face

Of my gauze window blow?

* *The poet shows his love of his native place by asking a trifling question.*

送元二使安西

王　维

渭城朝雨浥轻尘，
客舍青青柳色新。
劝君更尽一杯酒，
西出阳关无故人。

Seeing Yuan the Second Off to the Northwest Frontier

Wang Wei

No dust is raised on the road wet with morning rain;

The willows by the hotel look so fresh and green.

I invite you to drink a cup of wine again;

West of the Sunny Pass no more friends will be seen.

* *This is a most popular farewell song often sung at parting.*

九月九日忆山东兄弟

王　维

独在异乡为异客，
每逢佳节倍思亲。
遥知兄弟登高处，
遍插茱萸少一人。

Thinking of My Brothers on Mountain-climbing Day

Wang Wei

Alone, a lonely stranger in a foreign land,
I doubly pine for my kinsfolk on holiday.
I know my brothers would, with dogwood spray in hand,
Climb up the mountain and miss me so far away.

* *It was believed in China that to climb up mountains and carry dogwood spray on the ninth day of the ninth lunar month could drive evil spirits away.*

送别

王维

下马饮君酒，
问君何所之。
君言不得意，
归卧南山陲。
但去莫复问，
白云无尽时。

At Parting

Wang Wei

Dismounted, I drink with you
And ask what you've in view.
"I can't do what I will;
So I'll do what I will."
I'll ask you no more, friend,
Let clouds drift without end!

* *This poet speaks of their love of freedom at their parting.*

秋夜独坐

王 维

独坐悲双鬓，
空堂欲二更。
雨中山果落，
灯下草虫鸣。
白发终难变，
黄金不可成。
欲知除老病，
唯有学无生。

Sitting Alone on an Autumn Night

Wang Wei

Sitting alone, I grieve over my hair white;
In empty room it approaches midnight.
With the rain I hear in the mountain fruit fall;
By lamplight the insects chirp in my hall.
I cannot blacken my white hair while old,
Nor can I turn a metal into gold.
If you want to get rid of ills of old age,
You can only learn from the Buddhist sage.

* *The poet thinks it best to learn from the Buddhist sage.*

送梓州李使君

王　维

万壑树参天，
千山响杜鹃。
山中一夜雨，
树杪百重泉。
汉女输橦布，
巴人讼芋田。
文翁翻教授，
不敢倚先贤。

Seeing Li off to Zizhou

Wang Wei

The trees in your valley scrape the sky,
You'll hear in your hills cuckoo's cry.
If it rained at night in your mountain,
You'd see your tree tips hung like fountain.
Your women weave to make a suit;
You'd try to solve people's dispute.
The sage before you opened schools;
Like him you should carry out rules.

* *The poet describes Zizhou and advises his friend to be a good magistrate there.*

送秘书晁监还日本国

王　维

积水不可极，
安知沧海东！
九州何处远？
万里若乘空。
向国唯看日，
归帆但信风。
鳌身映天黑，
鱼眼射波红。
乡树扶桑外，
主人孤岛中。
别离方异域，
音信若为通！

Seeing Secretary Chao Back to Japan

Wang Wei

The sea is far and wide.
Who knows the other side?
How far is it away?
A thousand miles, you say.
Look at the sun, O please!
Your sail should trust the breeze.
Turtles bear the dark sky;
Giant fish raise waves high.
When you are in your isle,
There're trees from mile to mile.
Though we're separated for long,
Would you send me your song?

* *The poet imagines how his Japanese friend would cross the sea and go to his homeland.*

青溪

王维

言入黄花川，
每逐青溪水。
随山将万转，
趣途无百里。
声喧乱石中，
色静深松里。
漾漾泛菱荇，
澄澄映葭苇。
我心素已闲，
清川澹如此。
请留盘石上，
垂钓将已矣。

The Blue Stream

Wang Wei

I follow the Blue Rill
To the Stream of Yellow Blooms.
It winds from hill to hill
Till far away it looms.
It roars amid pebbles white
And calms down under pines green.
Weeds float on ripples light,
Reeds mirrored like a screen.
Mind's carefree, alone;
The clear stream flows with ease.
I would sit on a stone
To fish whatever I please.

* *This poem is typical of the poet's description of hills and rills. His mind is as carefree as the clear stream.*

山居秋暝

王　维

空山新雨后，
天气晚来秋。
明月松间照，
清泉石上流。
竹喧归浣女，
莲动下渔舟。
随意春芳歇，
王孙自可留。

Autumn Evening In The Mountains

Wang Wei

After fresh rain in mountains bare,

Autumn permeates evening air.

Among pine trees bright moonbeams peer;

Over crystal stones flows water clear.

Bamboos whisper of washer-maids;

Lotus stirs when fishing boat wades.

Though fragrant spring may pass away,

Still here's the place for you to stay.

* *This poem reveals the poet's love of nature (i. e. pine trees, whispering bamboos, lotus blooms; bright moonbeams, clear water, crystal stones.) and man (i. e. washermaids, fishermen.).*

使至塞上

王　维

单车欲问边，
属国过居延。
征蓬出汉塞，
归雁入胡天。
大漠孤烟直，
长河落日圆。
萧关逢候骑，
都护在燕然。

On Mission to the Frontier

Wang Wei

A single carriage goes to the frontier;
An envoy crosses northwest mountains high.
Like tumbleweed I leave the fortress drear;
As wild geese I come under Tartarian sky.
In boundless desert lonely smokes rise straight;
Over endless river the sun sinks round.
I meet a cavalier at the camp gate;
In northern fort the general will be found.

* *In 737 the poet was sent as an envoy to the frontier and he wrote this poem on his way, in which he compares himself to the rootless tumbleweed and the wild goose longing for home. This poem is well-known for the description of "straight" smoke and "round" sun against the background of a "boundless" desert and an "endless" river.*

出塞作

王　维

居延城外猎天骄，
白草连天野火烧。
暮云空碛时驱马，
秋日平原好射雕。
护羌校尉朝乘障，
破虏将军夜渡辽。
玉靶角弓珠勒马，
汉家将赐霍嫖姚。

Out of the Frontier

Wang Wei

The proud Tartar sons are hunting out of the town;

White grass spreads to the sky, wild fire bums up and down.

They ride on the desert when evening clouds hang low;

In autumn days on the vast plain they bend their bow.

Our officers strengthen the defense by daylight;

Our victorious generals cross the river at night.

The swords, bows and bridles mounted with gems and jade

Are awarded generals and their brave cavalcade.

* *This poem describes the Tartar forces and glorifies the Han generals defeating them.*

静夜思

李　白

床前明月光，
疑是地上霜。
举头望明月，
低头思故乡。

Thoughts on a Tranquil Night

Li Bai

Before my bed a pool of light—

O can it be frost on the ground?

Looking up, I find the moon bright;

Bowing, in homesickness I'm drowned.

* *Seeing a pool of moonlight, the poet is drowned in the pool of homesickness.*

峨眉山月歌

李　白

峨眉山月半轮秋，
影入平羌江水流。
夜发清溪向三峡，
思君不见下渝州。

The Moon over Mount Brow

Li Bai

The crescent moon looks like old Autumn's golden brow;
Its deep reflection flows with limpid water blue.
I'll leave the town on Clear Stream for the Three Gorges now.
O Moon, how I miss you when you are out of view!

* *This quatrain is written when the poet sails on the river between the steep cliffs which prevent him from seeing the moon he saw over Mount Brow in his homeland.*

望庐山瀑布

李　白

日照香炉生紫烟，
遥看瀑布挂前川。
飞流直下三千尺，
疑是银河落九天。

The Waterfall in Mount Lu Viewed from Afar

Li Bai

The sunlit Censer Peak exhales incense-like cloud;

Like an upended stream the cataract sounds loud.

Its torrent dashes down three thousand feet from high,

As if the Silver River fell from the blue sky.

* *This quatrain describes the beauty of the waterfall in Mount Lu with the Censer Peak above it. The poet compares it to the Silver River, Chinese name for the Milky Way.*

黄鹤楼送孟浩然之广陵

李　白

故人西辞黄鹤楼，
烟花三月下扬州。
孤帆远影碧空尽，
唯见长江天际流。

Seeing Meng Haoran off at Yellow Crane Tower

Li Bai

My friend has left the west where the Yellow Crane towers
For River Town green with willows and red with flowers.
His lessening sail is lost in the boundless blue sky,
Where I see but the endless River rolling by.

* *Meng leaves for the most beautiful town at the most beautiful time of the year.*

赠汪伦

李　白

李白乘舟将欲行，
忽闻岸上踏歌声。
桃花潭水深千尺，
不及汪伦送我情。

To Wang Lun

Li Bai

I, Li Bai, sit in a boat about to go,

When suddenly on shore your farewell songs overflow.

However deep the Lake of Peach Blossoms may be,

It's not so deep, O Wang Lun, as your love for me.

* *This is the poet's most popular farewell song.*

闻王昌龄左迁龙标遥有此寄

李　白

杨花落尽子规啼，
闻道龙标过五溪。
我寄愁心与明月，
随君直到夜郎西。

To Wang Changling Banished to the West

Li Bai

All willow-down has fallen and sad cuckoos cry

To hear you banished southwestward beyond Five Streams.

I would confide no sorrow to the moon on high

For it will follow you west of the Land of Dreams.

* *The only thing that could join the poet and his banished friend together is the moon.*

春夜洛城闻笛

李　白

谁家玉笛暗飞声，
散入春风满洛城。
此夜曲中闻折柳，
何人不起故园情。

Hearing the Flute on a Spring Night in Luoyang

Li Bai

From whose house has come the song of jade flute unseen?

It fills the town of Luoyang, spread by wind of spring.

Tonight I hear the farewell song of Willow Green.

To whom the tune will not nostalgic feeling bring?

* *It was a Chinese custom to break a twig of willow and present it to the parting friend, so the willow song has become a farewell song. On hearing it, the poet thinks of home.*

越中览古

李 白

越王勾践破吴归，
战士还家尽锦衣。
宫女如花满春殿，
只今唯有鹧鸪飞。

The Ruined Capital of Yue

Li Bai

The King of Yue returned, having destroyed the foe;
His loyal men came home, with silken dress aglow.
His palace thronged with flower-like ladies fair;
Now we see but a flock of partridges flying there.

* *The poet sighs over the ruined palace of the King of Yue who revenged his defeat by overthrowing the Kingdom of Wu.*

山中问答

李　白

问余何意栖碧山，
笑而不答心自闲。
桃花流水窅然去，
别有天地非人间。

A Reply

Li Bai

I dwell among green hills and someone asks me why;
My mind carefree, I smile and give him no reply.
Peach petals fallen on running water pass by,
This is an earthly paradise beneath the sky.

* *The poet prefers to live carefree in the hills or by the riverside.*

从军行

李 白

百战沙场碎铁衣，
城南已合数重围。
突营射杀呼延将，
独领残兵千骑归。

Song of a General after the Break-through

Li Bai

After a hundred battles, his armor is worn,

The southern town surrounded ring on ring in the morn.

When he breaks through and kills the chief of Tartar peers,

He comes back with a thousand beaten cavaliers.

* *This quatrain describes a general with his armor outworn and his cavaliers beaten after a breakthrough.*

春思

李白

燕草如碧丝，
秦桑低绿枝。
当君怀归日，
是妾断肠时。
春风不相识，
何事入罗帏？

A Faithful Wife Longing for Her Husband in Spring

Li Bai

Northern grass looks like green silk thread;

Western mulberries bend their head.

When you think of your home on your part,

Already broken is my heart.

Vernal wind, intruder unseen,

O how dare you part my bed screen!

* *The wife is so faithful to her husband that she would not allow the vernal wind to part her bed screen.*

清溪行

李　白

清溪清我心，
水色异诸水。
借问新安江，
见底何如此？
人行明镜中，
鸟度屏风里。
向晚猩猩啼，
空悲远游子。

Song of the Clear Stream

Li Bai

The Clear Stream clears my heart;
Its water flows apart.
I ask the River New,
"Why transparent are you?"
On mirror bright boats hie;
Between the screens birds fly.
At dusk the monkeys cry;
In vain the wayfarers sigh.

* *This poem describes the scenery on the Clear Stream and the poet's feeling on leaving it.*

送友人入蜀

李　白

见说蚕丛路，
崎岖不易行。
山从人面起，
云傍马头生。
芳树笼秦栈，
春流绕蜀城。
升沉应已定，
不必问君平。

To a Friend Parting for Shu

Li Bai

Rugged is the road, I hear,
Built by the pioneer.
In front steep mountains rise;
Beside my horse cloud flies.
Over plank way trees hang down;
Spring water girds the town.
Decided our rise and fall,
Do not bother at all!

* *This verse is descriptive as well as lyrical.*

鲁郡东石门送杜二甫

李　白

醉别复几日，
登临遍池台。
何时石门路，
重有金樽开。
秋波落泗水，
海色明徂徕。
飞蓬各自远，
且尽手中杯。

Farewell to Du Fu at Stone Gate

Li Bai

Before we part we've drunk for many days
And visited all the scenic spots and ways.
When at the Stone Gate shall we meet and drain
Our brimming golden cups of wine again?
The autumn waves of River Si still flow;
The seaside mountains stand in morning glow.
You'll go away as thistledown will fly.
So let us fill our cups and drink them dry.

* *This is a farewell song written by the romantic poet to the realistic poet.*

谢公亭

李　白

谢亭离别处，
风景每生愁。
客散青天月，
山空碧水流。
池花春映日，
窗竹夜鸣秋。
今古一相接，
长歌怀旧游。

Pavilion of Xie Tiao

Li Bai

Where the two poets parted,

The scene seems broken-hearted.

The moon's left in the sky;

The stream flows with deep sigh.

The pool reflects sunlight;

Bamboos shiver at night.

The present like the past;

Long, long will friendship last.

* *Xie Tiao (464—499) was a poet who parted with another poet at Xuancheng and built a pavilion there. Disfavored, he was put in jail and died in prison. Disgraced, Li Bai came to the pavilion and sighed for Xie's misfortune.*

塞下曲

李　白

五月天山雪，
无花只有寒。
笛中闻《折柳》，
春色未曾看。
晓战随金鼓，
宵眠抱玉鞍。
愿将腰下剑，
直为斩楼兰。

Frontier Song

Li Bai

In summer sky-high mountains white with snow,
In bitter cold no fragrant flowers blow.
Songs on the flute are heard of Willows Green,
But nowhere is the vernal color seen.
From dawn till dusk to beats of drums they fight;
With saddle in their arms they rest at night.
From scabbard at my waist I'd draw my sword
To kill the chieftain of the Turki horde.

* *The poet sympathizes with the warriors fighting in the bitter cold on the frontier.*

关山月

李　白

明月出天山，
苍茫云海间。
长风几万里，
吹度玉门关。
汉下白登道，
胡窥青海湾。
由来征战地，
不见有人还。
戍客望边色，
思归多苦颜。
高楼当此夜，
叹息未应闲。

The Moon over the Mountain Pass

Li Bai

From Heaven's Peak the moon rises bright
Over a boundless sea of cloud.
Winds blow for miles with main and might
Past the Jade Gate which stands so proud.
Our warriors march down the frontier,
While Tartars peer across Blue Bays.
From the battlefield outstretched here,
None have come back since olden days.
Guards watch the scene of borderland,
Thinking of home with wistful eyes.
Tonight upstairs their wives would stand,
Looking afar with longing sighs.

* *Seeing the moon, warriors on the frontier and their wives at home long for each other.*

夜泊牛渚怀古

李　白

牛渚西江夜，
青天无片云。
登舟望秋月，
空忆谢将军。
余亦能高咏，
斯人不可闻。
明朝挂帆席，
枫叶落纷纷。

Mooring at Night near Cattle Hill

Li Bai

I moor near Cattle Hill at night,
When there's no cloud to fleck the sky.
On deck I gaze at the moon bright,
Thinking of General Xie with a sigh.
I too can chant, to what avail?
None has like him a listening ear.
Tomorrow I shall hoist my sail,
Amid fallen leaves I'll leave here.

* *The poet thinks of General Xie who appreciated a poet chanting near Cattle Hill, but he can no longer find a connoisseur here now.*

古风（其二十四）

李　白

大车扬飞尘，
亭午暗阡陌。
中贵多黄金，
连云开甲宅。
路逢斗鸡者，
冠盖何辉赫。
鼻息干虹霓，
行人皆怵惕。
世无洗耳翁，
谁知尧与跖！

Eunuchs and Cock-fighters

Li Bai

The dust which eunuchs' carriages raise
Darkens at noon the public ways.
Of their gold the eunuchs are proud;
Their mansions rise to scrape the cloud.
I meet those who can make cocks fight,
With caps and cabs, so fair and bright.
Into rainbows they blow their breath,
Passers-by are frightened to death.
There is no connoisseur in this age.
Who can tell a thief from a sage?

* *The poet criticizes the rich and influential eunuchs and cock-fighters.*

寄东鲁二稚子

李　白

吴地桑叶绿，
吴蚕已三眠。
我家寄东鲁，
谁种龟阴田。
春事已不及，
江行复茫然。
南风吹归心，
飞堕酒楼前。
楼东一株桃，
枝叶拂青烟。
此树我所种，
别来向三年。

For My Two Children in East Lu

Li Bai

Mulberry leaves in Southern land are green;
The silkworms thrice in sleep must have been.
In Eastern Lu my family stays still.
Who'd help to sow our fields north of Lu Hill?
It's now too late to do farm work of spring.
What then am I to do while traveling?
The southern wind is blowing without stop;
My heart flies back to my old familiar wine-shop.
East of the shop there's a peach tree oft missed;
Its branches must be waving in bluish mist.
It is the tree I planted three years ago;

桃今与楼齐，
我行尚未旋。
娇女字平阳，
折花倚桃边。
折花不见我，
泪下如流泉。
小儿名伯禽，
与姊亦齐肩。
双行桃树下，
抚背复谁怜。
念此失次第，
肝肠日忧煎。
裂素写远意，
因之汶阳川。

If it has grown to reach the eaves, I don't know.

I have not been at home for three long years;

I can imagine my daughter appears

Beside the tree and plucks a flower pink,

Without seeing me, she must have, I think,

Shed copious tears.

My younger son has grown

Up to his sister's shoulders.

Beneath full-blown

Peach tree they stand side by side.

But who's there

To pat them on the back?

I feel, whene'er

I think of this, so painful that I write

And send to them this poem on silk white.

* *The poet shows his paternal love for his son and daughter in East Lu (Shandong).*

月下独酌四首（其一）

李　白

花间一壶酒，
独酌无相亲。
举杯邀明月，
对影成三人。
月既不解饮，
影徒随我身。
暂伴月将影，
行乐须及春。
我歌月徘徊，
我舞影零乱。
醒时同交欢，

Drinking Alone under the Moon (I)

Li Bai

Among the flowers, from a pot of wine
I drink without a companion of mine.
I raise my cup to invite the Moon who blends
Her light with my Shadow and we're three friends.
The Moon does not know how to drink her share;
In vain my Shadow follows me here and there.
Together with them for the time I stay,
And make merry before spring's spent away.
I sing and the Moon lingers to hear my song;
My Shadow's a mess while I dance along.
Sober, we three remain cheerful and gay;

醉后各分散。
永结无情游，
相期邈云汉。

Drunken, we part and each may go his way.

Our friendship will outshine all earthly love;

Next time we'll meet beyond the stars above.

* *The lonely poet thinks it happy to drink with the moon and his own shadow. His loneliness reveals his discontent with his actual life.*

拟古十二首（其九）

李　白

生者为过客，
死者为归人。
天地一逆旅，
同悲万古尘。
月兔空捣药，
扶桑已成薪。
白骨寂无言，
青松岂知春。
前后更叹息，
浮荣何足珍？

Life and Death

Li Bai

The living are but passers-by,

And those are going home who die.

The sky and earth are hotels just

For all to grieve over age-old dust.

The Moon Goddess lives long in vain;

The sacred tree's cut down with pain.

The bleached bones can nor speak nor sing.

Could green pines feel the warmth of spring?

Ancestors and posterity,

Don't prize but sigh for vanity!

* *This is a philosophical poem in which the poet equalizes life and death, imagines the sacred tree cut down, from which rose the sun, and sighs for the vanity of man.*

长干行

李 白

妾发初覆额，
折花门前剧。
郎骑竹马来，
绕床弄青梅。
同居长干里，
两小无嫌猜。
十四为君妇，
羞颜未尝开。
低头向暗壁，
千唤不一回。

Ballad of a Trader's Wife

Li Bai

My forehead barely covered by my hair,
Outdoors I plucked and played with flowers fair.
On hobby horse he came upon the scene;
Around the well we played with mumes still green.
We lived close neighbors on Riverside Lane,
Carefree and innocent, we children twain.
At fourteen years old I became his bride;
I often turned my bashful face aside.
Hanging my head, I'd look on the dark wall;
I would not answer his call upon call.

十五始展眉，
愿同尘与灰。
常存抱柱信，
岂上望夫台。
十六君远行，
瞿塘滟滪堆。
五月不可触，
猿声天上哀。
门前迟行迹，
一一生绿苔。
苔深不能扫，
落叶秋风早。
八月蝴蝶来，
双飞西园草。
感此伤妾心，

I was fifteen when I composed my brows;

To mix my dust with his were my dear vows.

Rather than break faith, he declared he'd die.

Who knew I'd live alone in tower high?

I was sixteen when he went far away,

Passing Three Gorges studded with rocks grey,

Where ships were wrecked when spring flood ran high,

Where gibbons' wails seemed coming from the sky.

Green moss now overgrows before our door;

His footprints, hidden, can be seen no more.

Moss can't be swept away, so thick it grows,

And leaves fall early when the west wind blows.

In yellow autumn butterflies would pass

Two by two in west garden over the grass.

The sight would break my heart and I'm afraid,

坐愁红颜老。
早晚下三巴，
预将书报家。
相迎不道远，
直至长风沙。

Sitting alone, my rosy cheeks would fade.

"O when are you to leave the western land?

Do not forget to tell me beforehand!

I'll walk to meet you and would not call it far

Even to go to Long Wind Beach where you are."

* *This ballad describes the love of a merchant's wife for her husband.*

登金陵凤凰台

李　白

凤凰台上凤凰游，
凤去台空江自流。
吴宫花草埋幽径，
晋代衣冠成古丘。
三山半落青天外，
一水中分白鹭洲。
总为浮云能蔽日，
长安不见使人愁。

The Phoenix Terrace at Jinling

Li Bai

On Phoenix Terrace once phoenixes came to sing;
The birds are gone but still roll on the river's waves.
The ruined palace's buried under weeds in spring;
The ancient sages in caps and gowns all lie in graves.
The three-peaked mountain is half lost in azure sky;
The two-forked stream by Egret Isle is kept apart.
As floating clouds can veil the bright sun from the eye,
Imperial Court now out of view saddens my heart.

* *The disgraced poet visits Phoenix Terrace and compares himself to a phoenix and the emperor to the bright sun veiled by floating clouds.*

乌栖曲

李白

姑苏台上乌栖时，
吴王宫里醉西施。
吴歌楚舞欢未毕，
青山欲衔半边日。
银箭金壶漏水多，
起看秋月坠江波。
东方渐高奈乐何！

Crows Flying Back to Their Nest

Li Bai

Over Royal Terrace when crows flew back to their nest,
The king in Royal Palace feasted his mistress drunk.
The Southern maidens sang and danced without a rest
Till beak-like mountain peaks would peck the sun half sunk.
The golden clepsydra could not stop water's flow,
Over the waves the autumn moon was hanging low.
Would not the king enjoy his fill in Eastern glow?

* *This is a satire on the King of Wu who held perpetual revelries with his favorite mistress in his Royal Palace in the 5th century BC.*

金陵城西楼月下吟

李　白

金陵夜寂凉风发，
独上高楼望吴越。
白云映水摇空城，
白露垂珠滴秋月。
月下沉吟久不归，
古来相接眼中稀。
解道澄江净如练，
令人长忆谢玄晖。

Orally Composed on the Western Tower of Jinling in Moonlight

Li Bai

The cool breeze blows on silent night in Town of Stone,

To view the south I mount the high tower alone.

White clouds and city walls mirrored on ripples swoon;

Dewdrops look like pearls dripping from the autumn moon.

Crooning long, I won't go back, drowned in moon rays;

How few are connoisseurs in my eyes since olden days!

Seeing the river crystal-clear and silver-white,

How I miss the unforgettable poet bright!

* *The poet gives free rein to his imagination in describing the scenery of Jinling or the Town of Stones: clouds could swoon, pearls could drip from the moon, and the poet could be drowned in moonlight. The unforgettable poet refers to Xie Tiao (464—499).*

蜀道难

李　白

噫吁嚱，危乎高哉！
蜀道之难，难于上青天！
蚕丛及鱼凫，
开国何茫然。
尔来四万八千岁，
不与秦塞通人烟。
西当太白有鸟道，
可以横绝峨眉巅。
地崩山摧壮士死，
然后天梯石栈相钩连。
上有六龙回日之高标，
下有冲波逆折之回川。

Hard is the Road to Shu

Li Bai

Oho! Behold! How Steep! How high!

The road to Shu is harder than to climb the sky.

Since the two pioneers

Put the kingdom in order,

Have passed forty-eight thousand years,

And few have tried to pass its border.

There's a bird track o'er Great White Mountain to the west,

Which cuts through Mountain Eyebrows by the crest.

The crest crumbled, five serpent-killing heroes slain,

Along the cliffs a rocky path was hacked then.

Above stand peaks too high for the sun to pass o'er;

Below the torrents run back and forth, churn and roar.

黄鹤之飞尚不得过，
猿猱欲度愁攀援。
青泥何盘盘，
百步九折萦岩峦。
扪参历井仰胁息，
以手抚膺坐长叹。
问君西游何时还，
畏途巉岩不可攀。
但见悲鸟号古木，
雄飞雌从绕林间。
又闻子规啼夜月，
愁空山，蜀道之难，
难于上青天，
使人听此凋朱颜。
连峰去天不盈尺，
枯松倒挂倚绝壁。
飞湍瀑流争喧豗，

Even the Golden Crane can't fly across;
How to climb over, gibbons are at a loss.
What tortuous mountain path Green Mud Ridge faces!
Around the top we turn nine turns each hundred paces.
Looking up breathless, I can touch the stars nearby;
Beating my breast, I sink aground with long, long sigh.
When will you come back from this journey to the west?
How can you climb up dangerous path and mountain crest,
Where you can hear on ancient trees but sad birds wail
And see the female birds fly, followed by the male?
And hear home-going cuckoos weep
Beneath the moon in mountains deep?
The road to Shu is harder than to climb the sky,
On hearing this, your cheeks would lose their rosy dye.
Between the sky and peaks there is not a foot's space,
And ancient pines hang, head down, from the cliff's surface.
And cataracts and torrents dash on boulders under,

砯崖转石万壑雷。
其险也如此，
嗟尔远道之人，胡为乎来哉！
剑阁峥嵘而崔嵬，
一夫当关，
万夫莫开。
所守或匪亲，
化为狼与豺。
朝避猛虎，夕避长蛇，
磨牙吮血，杀人如麻。
锦城虽云乐，
不如早还家。
蜀道之难，难于上青天，
侧身西望长咨嗟！

Roaring like thousands of echoes of thunder.

So dangerous these places are,

Alas! Why should you come here from afar?

Rugged is the path between the cliffs so steep and high,

Guarded by one

And forced by none.

Disloyal guards

Would turn wolves and pards,

Man-eating tigers at day-break

And at dusk blood-sucking long snake.

One may make merry in the Town of Silk, I know,

But I would rather homeward go.

The road to Shu is harder than to climb the sky,

I'd turn and westward look with long, long sigh.

* *This poem shows not only the hard way to Shu, present-day Sichuan Province, but also the hard way to rising above in society.*

宣州谢朓楼饯别校书叔云

李　白

弃我去者，
昨日之日不可留。
乱我心者，
今日之日多烦忧。
长风万里送秋雁，
对此可以酣高楼。
蓬莱文章建安骨，
中间小谢又清发。
俱怀逸兴壮思飞，
欲上青天揽明月。

Farewell to Uncle Yun, Imperial Librarian, at Xie Tiao's Pavilion in Xuancheng

Li Bai

What left me yesterday

Can be retained no more;

What troubles me today

Is the times for which I feel sore.

In autumn wind for miles and miles the wild geese fly.

Let's drink in face of this in the pavilion high!

Your writing's forcible like ancient poets while

Mine is in Junior Xie's clear and spirited style.

Both of us have an ideal high;

We would reach the moon in the sky.

抽刀断水水更流，
举杯消愁愁更愁。
人生在世不称意，
明朝散发弄扁舟。

Cut running water with a sword, it will faster flow;

Drink wine to drown your sorrow, it will heavier grow.

If we despair of all human affairs,

Let us roam in a boat with loosened hairs!

* *The poet complains to his uncle they could not fulfill their ideal in times of trouble.*

灞陵行送别

李　白

送君灞陵亭，
灞水流浩浩。
上有无花之古树，
下有伤心之春草。
我向秦人问路歧，
云是王粲南登之古道。
古道连绵走西京，
紫阙落日浮云生。
正当今夕断肠处，
骊歌愁绝不忍听。

Farewell at the Old Pavilion

Li Bai

We part at the Pavilion Old;

The river flows its water cold.

Above we see trees not in bloom,

Below the vernal grass in gloom.

I ask a wanderer if we go astray;

He says an ancient poet took this way.

The way extends to the west capital,

Where floating clouds at sunset veil the palace hall.

Heart-broken here and now I part with you.

How can we bear to hear songs of adieu?

* *The poet parts with his friend at the Old Pavilion by the riverside where Emperor Wen of the Han Dynasty was buried.*

行路难

李　白

大道如青天，
我独不得出。
羞逐长安社中儿，
赤鸡白狗赌梨栗。
弹剑作歌奏苦声，
曳裾王门不称情。
淮阴市井笑韩信，
汉朝公卿忌贾生。
君不见昔时燕家重郭隗，
拥彗折节无嫌猜。

Hard Is the Way of the World

Li Bai

The way is broad like the blue sky,

But no way out before my eye.

I am ashamed to follow those who have no guts,

Gambling on fighting cocks and dogs for pears and nuts.

Feng would go homeward way, having no fish to eat;

Zhou did not think to bow to noblemen was to meet.

General Han was mocked in the market place;

The brilliant scholar, Jia was banished in disgrace.

Have you not heard of King of Yan in days gone by, who venerated talents and built Terrace high

On which he offered gold to gifted men and stooped low and swept the floor to welcome them?

剧辛乐毅感恩分，
输肝剖胆效英才。
昭王白骨萦蔓草，
谁人更扫黄金台。
行路难，归去来。

Grateful, Ju Xin and Yue Yi came then

And served him heart and soul, both full of stratagem.

The king's bones were now buried, who would sweep the foot

And the Gold Terrace any more?

Hard is the way. Go back without delay!

* *The poet shows the way of the world was hard for talents like Feng, Zhou, Han, Jia. Only the King of Yan built a terrace to offer gold to talents, but he is no more now. So the poet says it would be better to go back without delay.*

日出入行

李　白

日出东方隈，
似从地底来。
历天又复入西海，
六龙所舍安在哉？
其始与终古不息，
人非元气，
安得与之久徘徊！
草不谢荣于春风，
木不怨落于秋天。
谁挥鞭策驱四运，
万物兴歇皆自然。
羲和！羲和！

Song of Sunrise and Sunset

Li Bai

From the east the sun comes around;

It seems to rise from underground.

Crossing the sky, it sinks in the sea of the west.

Where could the six dragons driving it take their rest?

It never changes from beginning to end.

Man is not a spirit,

Could he accompany it as a dear friend?

Grass will not for its growth thank the spring breeze;

Leaves won't complain of autumn when fallen from trees.

Who could drive summer and winter, autumn and spring?

Nature rules over rise and fall of everything.

O Driver of the Sun,

汝奚汩没于荒淫之波？
鲁阳何德，
驻景挥戈？
逆道违天，
矫诬实多。
吾将囊括大块，
浩然与溟涬同科。

What on the boundless waves have you done?

O Herculean Son,

How could you wield your spear to stop the Driver's run?

You go against the law divine.

What you do is quite out of line.

I would embrace the universe

To be one with Nature for better or for worse.

* *The legend went that the Driver of the Sun rode on six dragons, but the poet doubts it and jeers at the legendary Driver and the Herculean son who could stop his run. At last the poet would become one with Nature.*

江上吟

李　白

木兰之枻沙棠舟，
玉箫金管坐两头。
美酒樽中置千斛，
载妓随波任去留。
仙人有待乘黄鹤，
海客无心随白鸥。
屈平词赋悬日月，
楚王台榭空山丘。
兴酣落笔摇五岳，
诗成笑傲凌沧洲。
功名富贵若长在，
汉水亦应西北流。

Song on the River

Li Bai

In a ship of spice-wood with unsinkable oars,
Musicians at both ends, we drift along the shores.
We have sweet wine with singing girls to drink our fill,
And so the waves may carry us wherever they will.
Immortals could not fly without their yellow crane;
Unselfish men might follow white gulls to the main.
The verse of Qu Yuan shines as bright as sun and moon,
While palaces of Chu vanish like dreams at noon.
Seeing my pen in verve, even mountains shake;
Hearing my laughter proud, the seaside hermits wake.
If worldly fame and wealth were things to last forever,
Then northwestward would turn the eastward flowing river.

* *The romantic poet thinks himself as happy as immortals while roaming on the river.*

远别离

李　白

远别离，古有皇英之二女，
乃在洞庭之南，
潇湘之浦。
海水直下万里深，
谁人不言此离苦？
日惨惨兮云冥冥，
猩猩啼烟兮鬼啸雨。
我纵言之将何补？
皇穹窃恐不照余之忠诚，
雷凭凭兮欲吼怒。
尧舜当之亦禅禹。

Sorrow of Separation Severed for Aye

Li Bai

From the two princesses of ancient day,
Emperor Shun was buried south of the lake,
Where the two rivers meet awake,
And flow for miles and miles into the sea.
From the sorrow of separation who is free?
The sun is gloomy, veiled by dark cloud;
In mist and rain the monkeys wail and ghosts cry loud.
Of what avail is all that I say?
The Royal Dome knows not my loyalty;
Its thunder roars against me.
Even emperors to successors should give way.

君失臣兮龙为鱼，
权归臣兮鼠变虎。
或云：尧幽囚，舜野死。
九疑联绵皆相似，
重瞳孤坟竟何是？
帝子泣兮绿云间，
随风波兮去无还。
恸哭兮远望，
见苍梧之深山。
苍梧山崩湘水绝，
竹上之泪乃可灭。

When the king's not supported, the dragon turns into fish;

The rats in power become tigers as they with.

Emperor Yao was put in jail;

Emperor Shun died in the field to no avail.

Alike the Nine Mysterious Peaks look,

Where to find Emperor Shun's lonely tomb?

The princesses wept among the cloud green;

They gazed from afar and shed tears;

Now only the deep green mountain appears.

Only when mountains crumble and rivers go dry

Would the tear-specked bamboos vanish from the eye.

* *The legend goes that the two princesses were daughters of Emperor Yao and wives to Emperor Shun who died by the side of Dongting Lake and was buried at the foot of the Nine Mysterious Peaks. The princesses wept over the death of Emperor Shun and their tears specked the bamboos.*

长相思

李　白

长相思，在长安。
络纬秋啼金井阑，
微霜凄凄簟色寒。
孤灯不明思欲绝，
卷帷望月空长叹。
美人如花隔云端，[1]
上有青冥之高天，
下有渌水之波澜。
天长路远魂飞苦，
梦魂不到关山难。
长相思，摧心肝。

①英译文中漏译了此句。为尊重许渊冲先生译稿的原貌，漏译部分未作补充。

Endless Longing

Li Bai

I long for one in all at royal capital.

The autumn cricket wails beside the golden rails.

Light frost mingled with dew, my mat looks cold in hue.

My lonely lamp burns dull, of longing I would die;

Rolling up screens to view the moon, in vain I sigh.

Above, the boundless heaven spreads its canopy screen;

Below, the endless river rolls its billows green.

My soul can't fly over sky so vast nor streams so wide;

In dreams I can't go through mountain pass to her side.

We are so far apart; the longing breaks my heart.

* *The poet describes a woman's love for her lord in the capital. By tradition, the Beauty in a classical Chinese poem may refer to the sovereign. So it is said this poem reveals the poet's loyalty to the emperor.*

将进酒

李　白

君不见黄河之水天上来，
奔流到海不复回。
君不见高堂明镜悲白发，
朝如青丝暮成雪。
人生得意须尽欢，
莫使金樽空对月。
天生我材必有用，
千金散尽还复来。
烹羊宰牛且为乐，
会须一饮三百杯。
岑夫子，丹丘生，

Invitation to Wine

Li Bai

Do you not see the Yellow River come from the sky,
Rushing into the sea and ne'er come back?
Do you not see the mirrors bright in chambers high
Grieving o'er your snow-white hair though once it was silk-black?
When hopes are won, oh! Drink your fill in high delight,
And never leave your wine-cup empty in moonlight!
Heaven has made us talents, we're not made in vain.
A thousand gold coins spent, more will turn up again.
Kill a cow, cook a sheep and let us merry be,
And drink three hundred cupfuls of wine in high glee!
Dear friends of mine,

将进酒，杯莫停。
与君歌一曲，
请君为我倾耳听。
钟鼓馔玉不足贵，
但愿长醉不愿醒。
古来圣贤皆寂寞，
唯有饮者留其名。
陈王昔时宴平乐，
斗酒十千恣欢谑。
主人何为言少钱，
径须沽取对君酌。
五花马，千金裘，
呼儿将出换美酒，
与尔同销万古愁。

Cheer up, cheer up!

I invite you to wine. Do not put down your cup!

I will sing you a song, please hear,

O hear! Lend me a willing ear!

What difference will rare and costly dishes make?

I only want to get drunk and never to wake.

How many great men were forgotten through the ages?

But great drinkers are more famous than sober sages.

The Prince of Poets feast'd in his palace at will,

Drank wine at ten thousand a cask and laughed his fill.

A host should not complain of money he is short,

To drink with you I will sell things of any sort.

My fur coat worth a thousand coins of gold and my flower-dappled horse may be sold,

To buy good wine that we may drown the woes age-old.

* *The poet invites his friends to wine so as to drown the age-old sorrow.*

行路难

李 白

金樽清酒斗十千，
玉盘珍羞直万钱。
停杯投箸不能食，
拔剑四顾心茫然。
欲渡黄河冰塞川，
将登太行雪满山。
闲来垂钓碧溪上，
忽复乘舟梦日边。
行路难！行路难！
多歧路，今安在？
长风破浪会有时，
直挂云帆济沧海！

Hard is the Way of the World

Li Bai

Pure wine in golden cup costs ten thousand coins, good!
Choice dish in a jade plate is worth as much, nice food!
Pushing aside my cup and chopsticks. I can't eat;
Drawing my sword and looking round, I hear my heart beat.
I can't cross Yellow River: ice has stopped its flow;
I can't climb Mount Taihang: the sky is blind with snow.
I poise a fishing pole with ease on the green stream
Or set sail for the sun like the sage in a dream.
Hard is the way. Hard is the way.
Don't go astray! Whither today?
A time will come to ride the wind and cleave the waves;
I'll set my cloud-like sail to cross the sea which raves.

* *The poet sighs for the hard way of the world, but he will brave the wind and waves to cross the sea of perils.*

答王十二寒夜独酌有怀

李　白

昨夜吴中雪，
子猷佳兴发。
万里浮云卷碧山，
青天中道流孤月。
孤月沧浪河汉清，
北斗错落长庚明。
怀余对酒夜霜白，
玉床金井冰峥嵘。
人生飘忽百年内，
且须酣畅万古情。
君不能狸膏金距学斗鸡，

For Wang the Twelfth Who Drank Alone on a Cold Night

Li Bai

It snowed on southern shore last night;
You drank alone with keen delight.
Clouds float for miles and miles like rolled-up mountains high;
The lonely moon drifts in the midst of the sky.
The same lonely moon swims in Silver River dear;
The evening star is bright when Dipper stars appear.
You think of me drinking on a night white with frost;
The golden well with rails of jade in ice is lost.
Men live like floating clouds within a hundred years,
So we should drink our fill like our ancient compeers.
You cannot do as the eunuchs fond of cock fight,

坐令鼻息吹虹霓。
君不能学哥舒，
横行青海夜带刀，
西屠石堡取紫袍。
吟诗作赋北窗里，
万言不值一杯水。
世人闻此皆掉头，
有如东风射马耳。
鱼目亦笑我，
谓与明月同。
骅骝拳跼不能食，
蹇驴得志鸣春风。
《折杨》《黄华》合流俗，
晋君听琴枉《清角》。
《巴人》谁肯和《阳春》，
楚地犹来贱奇璞。
黄金散尽交不成，
白首为儒身被轻。

Who blow their breath like rainbow bright.
You cannot do as the general with sword in hand,
Who won his violet robe by slaughter on the land.
Writing verse or prose, by north window you remain;
Ten thousand words not worth a cup of water plain.
Hearing of this, people would turn their heads away,
Just as a horse with ears hurt by east wind would neigh.
The fish's eye mistaken for a pearl laughs at me,
Saying I cannot shine as the moon or as he.
A horse can't gallop when it has nothing to eat;
A donkey brays in spring breeze though crippled in fret.
The common people like to sing the vulgar thing.
How could the sacred lute please a secular king?
By popular musicians no fine music's played;
The Southerners usually look down on rare jade.
No friendship will be made when I've spent all my gold,
Though my hair turns white, I receive but glances cold.

一谈一笑失颜色，
苍蝇贝锦喧谤声。
曾参岂是杀人者？
谗言三及慈母惊。
与君论心握君手，
荣辱于余亦何有？
孔圣犹闻伤凤麟，
董龙更是何鸡狗！
一生傲岸苦不谐，
恩疏媒劳志多乖。
严陵高揖汉天子，
何必长剑拄颐事玉阶。
达亦不足贵，
穷亦不足悲。
韩信羞将绛、灌比，
祢衡耻逐屠沽儿。
君不见李北海，

My face has lost color when I speak in low voice;
For slanderers like flies make a deafening noise.
The sage's a murderer, how could that be believed?
The rumor thrice heard, the sage's mother was deceived.
We speak our bosom hand in hand and face to face.
What do I care about vain glory or disgrace?
Confucius only grieved no phoenix would appear.
Why should we hold these lower animals in fear?
Proud all my life long, with them I'm not in accord;
In disfavor, I'm alienated from the lord.
The hermit said to the emperor goodbye.
Why should he serve with his long sword in palace high?
The successful are not those we adore,
Nor the unsuccessful those we deplore.
General Han was ashamed of his compeers;
A loyal man despises one at whom he jeers.
Have you not seen Li of North Sea?

英风豪气今何在！
君不见裴尚书，
土坟三尺蒿棘居！
少年早欲五湖去，
见此弥将钟鼎疏。

Brave as he was, where now is he?

Have you not seen Secretary Pei

Buried among thorns? What to say?

While young, I wished to wander on the lake;

Now older, born the dreams of glory I'm awake.

* *The poet talks about his friendship, his despise of slanderers, his love for the hermit and the loyal general, his sympathy with Li and Pei unjustly punished by the prime minister, and his wish to wander on the lake like General Fan with the Beauty in 473 BC.*

八阵图

杜 甫

功盖三分国，
名成八阵图。
江流石不转，
遗恨失吞吴。

The Stone Fortress

Du Fu

With his exploits history is crowned;
For the stone fortress he's renowned.
The river flows but stones still stand,
Though he'd not taken back lost land.

* *The stone fortress was the exploit of Zhuge Liang, premier of the Kingdom of Shu.*

绝 句

杜 甫

两个黄鹂鸣翠柳，
一行白鹭上青天。
窗含西岭千秋雪，
门泊东吴万里船。

A Quatrain

Du Fu

Two golden orioles sing amid the willows green;

A flock of white egrets fly into the blue sky.

My window frames the snow-crowned western mountain scene;

My door off says to eastward going ships "Goodbye!"

* *The first couplet of this quatrain is a colorful picture: golden orioles and green willows, white egrets and blue sky. The second couplet presents a vast view of the east and the west, mountain and river, but within the framework of his door and window.*

望岳

杜甫

岱宗夫如何？
齐鲁青未了。
造化钟神秀，
阴阳割昏晓。
荡胸生层云，
决眦入归鸟。
会当凌绝顶，
一览众山小。

Gazing on Mount Tai

Du Fu

O peak of peaks, how high it stands!
One boundless green overspreads two States.
A marvel done by Nature's hands,
Over light and shade it dominates.
Clouds rise therefrom and lave my breast;
I stretch my eyes to see birds fleet.
I will ascend the mountain's crest;
It dwarfs all peaks under my feet.

* *Gazing on Mount Tai, the poet seems to ascend in and dwarf all peaks under his feet.*

春望

杜甫

国破山河在，
城春草木深。
感时花溅泪，
恨别鸟惊心。
烽火连三月，
家书抵万金。
白头搔更短，
浑欲不胜簪。

Spring View

Du Fu

On war-torn land streams flow and mountains stand;

In vernal town grass and weeds are overgrown.

Grieved over the years, flowers make us shed tears;

Hating to part, hearing birds breaks our heart.

The beacon fire has gone higher and higher;

Words from household are worth their weight in gold.

I cannot bear to scratch my grizzled hair;

It grows too thin to hold a light hairpin.

* *This poem with inner rhymes shows the poet's love of his country and his family.*

江　汉

杜　甫

江汉思归客，
乾坤一腐儒。
片云天共远，
永夜月同孤。
落日心犹壮，
秋风病欲苏。
古来存老马，
不必取长途。

On River Han

Du Fu

On River Han my home thoughts fly,
Bookworm with worldly ways in fright.
The cloud and I share the vast sky;
I'm lonely as the moon all night.
My heart won't sink with sinking sun;
West wind blows my illness away.
A jaded horse may not have done,
Though it cannot go a long way.

* *The poet compares himself to a jaded horse which can still run but not a long way.*

月　夜

杜　甫

今夜鄜州月，
闺中只独看。
遥怜小儿女，
未解忆长安。
香雾云鬟湿，
清辉玉臂寒。
何时倚虚幌，
双照泪痕干。

A Moonlit Night

Du Fu

On the moon over Fuzhou which shines bright,
Alone you would gaze in your room tonight.
I'm grieved to think our little children dear
Too young to yearn for their old father here.
Your cloudlike hair is moist with dew, it seems;
Your jade-white arms would feel the cold moonbeams.
O when can we stand by the window side,
Watching the moon with our tear traces dried?

* *As a refugee, the poet writes this poem to his wife far away in Qiang Village at Fuzhou.*

春夜喜雨

杜 甫

好雨知时节，
当春乃发生。
随风潜入夜，
润物细无声。
野径云俱黑，
江船火独明。
晓看红湿处，
花重锦官城。

Happy Rain on a Spring Night

Du Fu

Good rain knows its time right,
It will fall when comes spring.
With wind it steals in night;
Mute, it wets everything.
Over wild lanes dark cloud spreads;
In boat a lantern looms.
Dawn sees saturated reds;
The town's heavy with blooms.

* *The spring rain personified gladdens the poet for it knows the right time to fall, moistens everything and lasts long. The poet tells us what he hears, sees and thinks on a rainy night.*

日暮

杜　甫

牛羊下来久，
各已闭柴门。
风月自清夜，
江山非故园。
石泉流暗壁，
草露滴秋根。
头白灯明里，
何须花烬繁。

After Sunset

Du Fu

The sheep and cattle come to rest,

All thatched gates closed east and west.

The gentle breeze and the moon bright

Remind me of homeland at night.

Among rocks flow fountains unseen;

Autumn drips dewdrops on grass green.

The candle brightens white-haired head.

Why should its flame blaze up so red?

* *This poem was written in 767 when the poet had left his homeland for several years. As he was in a gloomy mood, he did not like the candlelight to brighten the dark corner of his heart. His nostalgia is intensified by the contrast between the outer world and his inner world.*

孤雁

杜甫

孤雁不饮啄，
飞鸣声念群。
谁怜一片影，
相失万重云？
望尽似犹见，
哀多如更闻。
野鸦无意绪，
鸣噪自纷纷。

The Lonely Swan

Du Fu

The lonely swan won't drink nor eat,
But longs to join its flock to fleet.
Who will pity its shadow lonely,
Astray in the clouds, it wails only.
Out of sight, still it seems in view;
Lost in grief, its song's heard anew.
What do insensible birds know?
You hear only caws of the crow.

* *This is the song of a lonely swan longing for its flock.*

春日忆李白

杜　甫

白也诗无敌，
飘然思不群。
清新庾开府，
俊逸鲍参军。
渭北春天树，
江东日暮云。
何时一樽酒，
重与细论文。

Thinking of Li Bai on a Spring Day

Du Fu

Li Bai is unrivalled in verse;

He towers in the universe.

Fresher than Yu on northern shore;

Brighter than Bao, poet of yore.

I long for him as longing tree;

At sunset will he think of me?

When may we drink a cup of wine

And talk about prose and verse fine?

* *Du Fu in the north thinks of Li Bai in the south and compares him to two poets of yore.*

月夜忆舍弟

杜　甫

戍鼓断人行，
边秋一雁声。
露从今夜白，
月是故乡明。
有弟皆分散，
无家问死生。
寄书长不达，
况乃未休兵。

Thinking of My Brothers on a Moonlit Night

Du Fu

War drums break people's journey drear;

A swan honks on autumn frontier.

Dew turns into frost since tonight;

The moon viewed from home is more bright.

I've brothers scattered here and there;

For our life or death none would care.

Letters can't reach where I intend;

Alas! The war's not come to an end.

* *The poet sighs for his brothers cannot get together in time of war.*

羌村三首（其一）

杜　甫

峥嵘赤云西，
日脚下平地。
柴门鸟雀噪，
归客千里至。
妻孥怪我在，
惊定还拭泪。
世乱遭飘荡，
生还偶然遂。
邻人满墙头，
感叹亦歔欷。
夜阑更秉烛，
相对如梦寐。

Coming Back to Qiang Village (I)

Du Fu

Like rugged hills hangs gilt-edged cloud;
The sunset sheds departing ray.
The wicket gate with birds is loud,
When I come back from far away.
At my appearance starts my wife;
Then calming down, she melts in tears.
Happy, I come back still in life,
While people drift in bitter years.
My neighbors look over the wall;
They sigh and from their eyes tears stream.
When night comes, candles light the hall;
We sit face to face as in dream.

* *This poem describes the reunion of the poet's family at Qiang Village.*

禹庙

杜甫

禹庙空山里，
秋风落日斜。
荒庭垂橘柚，
古屋画龙蛇。
云气嘘青壁，
江声走白沙。
早知乘四载，
疏凿控三巴。

Temple of Emperor Yu

Du Fu

Your temple stands in empty hills,
The autumn breeze with sunset fills.
Oranges still hang in your courtyard;
Dragons on your old walls breathe hard.
Over green cliff float clouds in flight;
The river washes the sand white.
On water as on land you'd go
To dredge the streams and make them flow.

* *Emperor Yu was said to have stemmed the flood about 2000 BC.*

前出塞（其六）

杜　甫

挽弓当挽强，
用箭当用长。
射人先射马，
擒贼先擒王。
杀人亦有限，
立国自有疆。
苟能制侵陵，
岂在多杀伤？

Songs of the Frontier (VI)

Du Fu

The bow you carry should be strong;

The arrows you use should be long.

Shoot before a horseman his horse;

Capture the chief to beat his force,

Slaughter shan't go beyond its sphere;

Each State should guard its own frontier.

If an invasion is repelled,

Why shed more blood unless compelled?

* *The poet speaks of the art of war and his love of peace.*

房兵曹胡马

杜　甫

胡马大宛名，
锋棱瘦骨成。
竹批双耳峻，
风入四蹄轻。
所向无空阔，
真堪托死生。
骁腾有如此，
万里可横行。

General Fang's Steed

Du Fu

The steed from the barbaric west
Has angular frame and strong chest.
Like pointed bamboo its sharp ear,
As swift wind its fleet hoofs, O hear!
The way it runs will never end;
Life or death on it may depend.
When you have such a fiery steed,
You can ride where you will indeed.

* *The poet writes this poem in praise of the fiery steed of General Fang.*

奉赠韦左丞丈二十二韵

杜　甫

纨绔不饿死，
儒冠多误身。
丈人试静听，
贱子请具陈：
甫昔少年日，
早充观国宾。
读书破万卷，
下笔如有神。
赋料扬雄敌，
诗看子建亲。
李邕求识面，

For Minister Wei

Du Fu

The rich of hunger never die;
The poor of their misfortune sigh.
Minister Wei, would you please hear
What I would confide to your ear?
While young, I was a candidate
In Civil Exams of the State.
Having ten thousand volumes read,
I wrote as if by God I was led.
In prose I was second to none;
In verse I vied with the best one.
Ministers would like to know me,

王翰愿卜邻。
自谓颇挺出，
立登要路津。
致君尧舜上，
再使风俗淳。
此意竟萧条，
行歌非隐沦。
骑驴十三载，
旅食京华春。
朝扣富儿门，
暮随肥马尘。
残杯与冷炙，
到处潜悲辛。
主上顷见征，
欻然欲求伸。
青冥却垂翅，
蹭蹬无纵鳞。

And poets my neighbors would be.
I thought, outstanding as was I,
A job was not hard to come by.
I would help the crown in my strife
To purify the ways of life.
I could not do what I desired;
Singing, I would not be retired.
Riding a donkey thirteen years,
I suffered the capital's sneers.
I knock at the mansions by day;
At dusk I hear dusty steeds neigh.
I eat leftovers of a meal;
In vain I suffer a great deal.
The Crown showed his favor and love;
I saw a chance to rise above.
In the sky the roc folds its wings;
On the sea swim no scaly kings.

甚愧丈人厚，
甚知丈人真。
每于百僚上，
猥诵佳句新。
窃效贡公喜，
难甘原宪贫。
焉能心怏怏，
只是走踆踆。
今欲东入海，
即将西去秦。
尚怜终南山，
回首清渭滨。
常拟报一饭，
况怀辞大臣。
白鸥没浩荡，
万里谁能驯！

I thank you for your kindness true,

Knowing you're kind in what you do.

Whenever you meet a good friend,

It's my new verse you recommend.

Though glad of your prosperity,

How could I bear my poverty?

I'm not unhappy in my place;

But it's a dilemma I face.

Should I go seaward for my rest,

Or to the capital in the west?

I love the Southern Mountains high

And the clear River flowing by.

I can't forget what I owe you,

Nor what to ministers is due.

Like a white gull on the vast sea,

I'd fly for miles and miles, carefree.

* *The poet thanks Minister Wei for his kind help but he would be free like a gull.*

江　村

杜　甫

清江一曲抱村流，
长夏江村事事幽。
自去自来梁上燕，
相亲相近水中鸥。
老妻画纸为棋局，
稚子敲针作钓钩。
多病所须唯药物，
微躯此外更何求？

The Riverside Village

Du Fu

See the clear river wind by the village and flow!
We pass the long summer by riverside with ease.
The swallows freely come in and freely out go.
The gulls on water snuggle each other as they please.
My wife draws lines on paper to make a chessboard;
My son bends a needle into a fishing hook.
Ill, I need only medicine I can afford.
What else do I want for myself in my humble nook?

* *This poem describes the thatched hall built in 760 and the leisurely life of the poet.*

燕子来舟中作

杜　甫

湖南为客动经春，
燕子衔泥两度新。
旧入故园尝识主，
如今社日远看人。
可怜处处巢居室，
何异飘飘托此身。
暂语船樯还起去，
穿花贴水益沾巾。

To the Swallow Coming to My Boat

Du Fu

Another spring in boat I stay;
Again swallows peck clods of clay.
You know me in my native land;
Now gazing from afar you stand.
Ah, here and there you build your nest;
Now and again I find no rest.
You greet me and then leave the mast;
My tears stream down to see you past.

* *This poem presents a contrast between the swallow building its nest and the poet who could not go home.*

悲陈陶

杜　甫

孟冬十郡良家子，
血作陈陶泽中水。
野旷天清无战声，
四万义军同日死。
群胡归来血洗箭，
仍唱胡歌饮都市。
都人回面向北啼，
日夜更望官军至。

Lament on the Defeat at Chentao

Du Fu

In early winter noble sons of household good
Blended with water in Chentao mires their pure blood.
No more war cry under the sky on the vast plain,
In one day forty thousand loyal warriors slain.
The enemy came back with blood-stained arrows long;
They drank in market place and shouted barbarous song.
Our countrymen turned north their faces bathed in tears;
Day and night they expect the royal cavaliers.

* *The poet weeps over the forty thousand men slain by the rebels in Chentao and expects in vain the recovery of the lost land by the royal forces.*

登高

杜甫

风急天高猿啸哀，
渚清沙白鸟飞回。
无边落木萧萧下，
不尽长江滚滚来。
万里悲秋常作客，
百年多病独登台。
艰难苦恨繁霜鬓，
潦倒新停浊酒杯。

On the Height

Du Fu

The wind so swift, the sky so wide, apes wail and cry;
Water so clear and beach so white, birds wheel and fly.
The boundless forest sheds its leaves shower by shower;
The endless river rolls its waves hour after hour.
A thousand miles from home, I'm grieved at autumn's plight;
Ill now and then for years, alone I'm on this height.
Living in times so hard, at frosted hair I pine;
Cast down by poverty, I have to give up wine.

* *This is the most balanced verse in Tang poetry.*

曲江二首（其一）

杜　甫

一片花飞减却春，
风飘万点正愁人。
且看欲尽花经眼，
莫厌伤多酒入唇。
江上小堂巢翡翠，
苑边高冢卧麒麟。
细推物理须行乐，
何用浮名绊此身？

The Winding River (I)

Du Fu

Spring fades when petals on petals fly as they please;
It grieves me to see dots on dots waft in the breeze.
Enjoy the blooms passing away before your eyes;
Do not refuse to drown your grief in wine and sighs!
In the riverside halls kingfishers build their nest;
Before the tomb the stone animals lie at rest.
The law of Nature tells us to enjoy as we may.
Why spoil our joy by sheer vanity of the day?

* *The poet tells us to enjoy delight on the Winding River while we may.*

曲江二首（其二）

杜　甫

朝回日日典春衣，
每日江头尽醉归。
酒债寻常行处有，
人生七十古来稀。
穿花蛱蝶深深见，
点水蜻蜓款款飞。
传语风光共流转，
暂时相赏莫相违。

The Winding River (II)

Du Fu

Back from the court from day to day, I pawn spring gown.
To get drunk by the riverside where I go down.
In every wine shop I have a debt to pay;
It's rare to live to seventy since olden day.
Deeper and deeper amid flowers go butterflies;
Slowly and slowly on water skim dragonflies.
I will enjoy the present with those on the wing.
Do not let pass away any delightful thing!

* *The poet tells us how he enjoys delight in poverty.*

咏怀古迹五首（其二）

杜　甫

摇落深知宋玉悲，
风流儒雅亦吾师。
怅望千秋一洒泪，
萧条异代不同时。
江山故宅空文藻，
云雨荒台岂梦思？
最是楚宫俱泯灭，
舟人指点到今疑。

The Poet Song Yu's Abode

Du Fu

When leaves shiver and fall, I see the poet drear;
Gallant and elegant, he is my master dear.
Looking back a thousand springs, can I not shed tears?
Desolate for long, we are not of the same years.
His autumn song's left in his old home by the stream.
Did clouds bring showers for flowers in the king's dream?
Even the royal palace falls now in decay,
The boatman points to the ruins in doubt today.

* *Song Yu (298 BC—222 BC) was famous for his Ode to Autumn (when leaves shiver and fall) and his Goddess of Mount Witch (who brings showers for thirsting flowers).*

咏怀古迹五首（其五）

杜　甫

诸葛大名垂宇宙，
宗臣遗像肃清高。
三分割据纡筹策，
万古云霄一羽毛。
伯仲之间见伊吕，
指挥若定失萧曹。
运移汉祚终难复，
志决身歼军务劳。

To the Prime Minister of Shu

Du Fu

Your fame spreads far and wide, honored for long, long time:

Your noble image looks so solemn and sublime.

The world divided into three, Shu in the west;

You drove all clouds away with a plume on the crest.

You could rival all premiers of the olden day;

Beside you, all generals look pale and fade away.

But the kingdom at stake, you could not turn the tide;

Busy with your campaigns, with labor lost you died.

* *The Prime Minister refers to Zhuge Liang in the time of the Three Kingdoms (220—280).*

蜀相

杜甫

丞相祠堂何处寻？
锦官城外柏森森。
映阶碧草自春色，
隔叶黄鹂空好音。
三顾频烦天下计，
两朝开济老臣心。
出师未捷身先死，
长使英雄泪满襟。

Temple of the Premier of Shu

Du Fu

The Premier's Temple's in the shade
Of cypress woven with brocade.
The steps are green with grass in spring;
In vain amid leaves orioles sing.
Consulted thrice on state affair,
He served two reigns beyond compare.
He died before he won success.
Could heroes' tears not wet their dress?

* *The premier of Shu was Zhuge Liang (181—234) and the Town of Brocade is Chengdu.*

诸将五首（其二）

杜　甫

韩公本意筑三城，
拟绝天骄拔汉旌。
岂谓尽烦回纥马，
翻然远救朔方兵。
胡来不觉潼关隘，
龙起犹闻晋水清。
独使至尊忧社稷，
诸君何以答升平？

Five Generals (II)

Du Fu

The Duke of Han planned to build three victorious walls
To stop the foe from coming near our capitals.
Could he anticipate the Western cavaliers,
After their victory, would not leave Northern frontiers?
The Pass could not prevent the foe from coming near;
After the dragon's rise, we can see our land clear.
Should the sovereign worry about the country's fate,
Generals could not have done their duty for the State.

* *The poet praises the Duke of Han who has built three victors' walls, and criticizes other generals who cannot stop the enemy's invasion on Northern frontiers. The dragon refers to the new sovereign who has recaptured the Western capital.*

饮中八仙歌

杜　甫

知章骑马似乘船，
眼花落井水底眠。
汝阳三斗始朝天，
道逢曲车口流涎，
恨不移封向酒泉。
左相日兴费万钱，
饮如长鲸吸百川，
衔杯乐圣称避贤。
宗之潇洒美少年，
举觞白眼望青天，
皎如玉树临风前。

Song of Eight Immortal Drinkers

Du Fu

Zhizhang feels dizzy on his horse as in a boat.

Should he fall into the well, asleep there he should float.

Prince Li Jin would go to court after drinking three jars;

His mouth would water, seeing wine-transporting cars.

He would have as his fief the Spring of Wine in dreams.

Left Minister buys wine with thousand coins by day,

He would drink like a whale a hundred streams,

Dismissed now, he would drink impure wine as he may.

Without restraint, Zongzhi is a gallant young guy.

Wine cup in hand, he turns white eyes to the blue sky.

Like one of the jade trees standing in vernal breeze.

苏晋长斋绣佛前，
醉中往往爱逃禅。
李白斗酒诗百篇，
长安市上酒家眠。
天子呼来不上船，
自称臣是酒中仙。
张旭三杯草圣传，
脱帽露顶王公前，
挥毫落纸如云烟。
焦遂五斗方卓然，
高谈雄辩惊四筵。

The Buddhist Su Jin should neither drink nor eat the meat,
But drunk, to run away from Buddha he is fleet.
Li Bai would turn sweet nectar into verses fine.
Drunk in the capital, he'd lie in shops of wine.
Even imperial summons proudly he'd decline,
Saying immortals could leave the drink divine.
In cursive writing Zhang Xu's worthy of his fame.
After three drinks he bares his head before lord and dame,
And splashes cloud and mist on paper as with flame.
Jiao Sui is sober after drinking jar on jar;
His eloquence astonishes guests near and far.

* *The poet describes eight drinkers: He Zhizhang who writes Home-Coming. Prince Li Jin, the Left Minister, Zuo Zongzhi for whom Li Bai writes Farewell to a Friend, a Buddhist who worships wine more than Buddha, Li Bai who could turn wine into verse, Zhang Xu who paints better when drinks, and Jiao Sui more eloquent after drinking.*

哀江头

杜　甫

少陵野老吞声哭，
春日潜行曲江曲。
江头宫殿锁千门，
细柳新蒲为谁绿。
忆昔霓旌下南苑，
苑中万物生颜色。
昭阳殿里第一人，
同辇随君侍君侧。
辇前才人带弓箭，
白马嚼啮黄金勒。
翻身向天仰射云，
一笑正坠双飞翼。

Lament along the Winding River

Du Fu

Old and deprived, I swallow tears on a spring day;
Along Winding River in stealth I go my way.
All palace gates and doors are locked on river shore;
Willows and reeds are green for no one to adore.
I remember rainbow banners streamed at high tide
To Southern Park where everything was beautified.
The first lady of the Sunny Palace would ride
In the imperial chariot by the emperor's side.
The horsewomen before her bore arrows and bow;
Their white steeds champed at golden bits on the front row.
One archer, leaning back, shot at cloud in the sky;
One arrow brought down two winged birds from on high.

明眸皓齿今何在？
血污游魂归不得。
清渭东流剑阁深，
去住彼此无消息。
人生有情泪沾臆，
江水江花岂终极！
黄昏胡骑尘满城，
欲往城南望城北。

Where are the first lady's pearly teeth and eyes bright?

Her spirit, blood-stained, could not come back from the height.

Far from Sword Cliff, with River Wei her soul flew east;

The emperor got no news from her in the least.

A man who has a heart will wet his breast with tears.

Would riverside grass and flowers not weep for years?

At dusk the rebels' horses overrun the town;

I want to go upward, but instead I go down.

* *The poet laments over the Winding River where the Bright Emperor made pleasure with his favorite Lady Yang who is dead, and where the rebels are running riot.*

兵车行

杜　甫

车辚辚，马萧萧，
行人弓箭各在腰。
耶娘妻子走相送，
尘埃不见咸阳桥。
牵衣顿足拦道哭，
哭声直上干云霄。
道傍过者问行人，
行人但云点行频。
或从十五北防河，
便至四十西营田。
去时里正与裹头，
归来头白还戍边。

Song of the Conscripts

Du Fu

The conscripts march with bow and arrows at the waist.

Their fathers, mothers, wives and children come in haste

To see them off; the bridge is shrouded in dust they've raised.

They clutch at their coats, stamp the feet and bar the way;

Their grief cries loud and strikes the cloud straight, straight away.

An onlooker by roadside asks an enrollee.

"The conscription is frequent," only answers he.

Some went north at fifteen to guard the river shore,

And were sent west to till the land at forty.

The elder bound their young heads when they went away;

Just home, they're sent to the frontier though their hair's gray.

边庭流血成海水，
武皇开边意未已。
君不闻汉家山东二百州，
千村万落生荆杞。
纵有健妇把锄犁，
禾生陇亩无东西。
况复秦兵耐苦战，
被驱不异犬与鸡。
长者虽有问，
役夫敢申恨。
且如今年冬，
未休关西卒。
县官急索租，
租税从何出。
信知生男恶，
反是生女好。
生女犹是嫁比邻，

The field on borderland becomes a sea of blood;

The emperor's greed for land is still at high flood.

Have you not heard two hundred districts east of the Hua
Mountains lie,

Where briers and brambles grow in villages far and nigh?

Although stout women can wield the plough and the hoe,

Thorns and weeds in the east as in the west o'ergrow.

The enemy are used to hard and stubborn fight;

Our men are driven just like dogs or fowls in flight.

You are kind to ask me

To complain I'm not free.

In winter of this year

Conscription goes on here.

The magistrates for taxes press.

How can we pay them in distress?

If we had known sons bring no joy,

We would have preferred girl to boy.

A daughter can be wed to a neighbor, alas!

生男埋没随百草。
君不见青海头，
古来白骨无人收。
新鬼烦冤旧鬼哭，
天阴雨湿声啾啾。

A son can only be buried under the grass?

Have you not seen on borders green

Bleached bones since olden days unburied on the plain?

The old ghosts weep and cry, while the new ghosts complain;

The air is loud with screech and scream in gloomy rain.

* *The poet criticizes the Bright Emperor of the Tang Dynasty for his conscription of soldiers in war.*

丽人行

杜　甫

三月三日天气新，
长安水边多丽人。
态浓意远淑且真，
肌理细腻骨肉匀。
绣罗衣裳照暮春，
蹙金孔雀银麒麟。
头上何所有，
翠为㔩叶垂鬓唇。
背后何所见，
珠压腰衱稳称身。
就中云幕椒房亲，
赐名大国虢与秦。

Satire on Fair Ladies

Du Fu

The weather's fine in the third moon on the third day,

By riverside so many beauties in array.

Each of the ladies has a fascinating face,

Their skin is delicate, their manner full of grace.

Embroidered with peacocks and unicorns in gold,

Their dress in rich silks shines so bright when spring is old.

What do they wear on the head?

Emerald pendant leaves hang down in silver thread.

What do you see from behind?

How nice-fitting are their waist bands with pearls combined.

Among them there're the emperor's favorite kin,

Ennobled Duchess of Guo comes with Duchess of Qin.

紫驼之峰出翠釜，
水精之盘行素鳞。
犀箸厌饫久未下，
鸾刀缕切空纷纶。
黄门飞鞚不动尘，
御厨络绎送八珍。
箫鼓哀吟感鬼神，
宾从杂沓实要津。
后来鞍马何逡巡，
当轩下马入锦茵。
杨花雪落覆白苹，
青鸟飞去衔红巾。
炙手可热势绝伦，
慎莫近前丞相嗔。

What do they eat?

The purple meat of camels hump cooked in green cauldron as a dish;

On crystal plate is served snow-white slices of raw fish.

See rhino chopsticks the satiated eaters stay,

And untouched morsels carved by belled knives on the tray.

When eunuchs' horses come running, no dust is raised;

They bring still more rare dishes delicious to the taste.

Listen to soul-stirring music of flutes and drums!

On the main road an official retinue comes.

A rider ambles on saddled horse, the last of all,

He alights, treads on satin carpet, enters the hall.

The willow down-like snow falls on the duckweed white;

The blue bird picking red handkerchief goes in flight.

The prime minister's powerful without a peer.

His angry touch would bum your hand. Do not come near!

* *This is a satire against the emperor's favorite Lady Yang and her sisters and their brother who became the Prime Minister. The poet describes their beauty, their dress, their food. He hints at the incest by the frivolous willow-down and the blue bird which carries secret amorous message for them.*

春山夜月

于良史

春山多胜事，
赏玩夜忘归。
掬水月在手，
弄花香满衣。
兴来无远近，
欲去惜芳菲。
南望鸣钟处，
楼台深翠微。

The Vernal Hill in Moonlit Night

Yu Liangshi

How much delight in vernal hill?
Don't go back but enjoy your fill!
Drinking water, you drink moonbeams;
Plucking flowers, you pluck sweet dreams.
Happy, you would forget the hours;
About to go, you can't leave flowers.
Looking south where you hear the bell,
You'll find green bowers in green dell.

* *This poem describes the exquisite delight in the vernal hill where moonbeams dissolve into the handful of water the poet drinks.*

咏 柳

贺知章

碧玉妆成一树高，
万条垂下绿丝绦。
不知细叶谁裁出，
二月春风似剪刀。

The Willow

He Zhizhang

The slender beauty's dressed in emerald all about;
A thousand branches droop like fringes made of jade.
But do you know by whom these slim leaves are cut out?
The wind of early spring is sharp as scissor blade.

* *This is a fine picture of the willow in which the imaginative poet compares the tree to a beautiful woman dressed in emerald and its branches to the fringes of her skirt, and its slim leaves cut by the sharp wind as by the scissor blade.*

回乡偶书二首（其一）

贺知章

少小离家老大回，
乡音无改鬓毛衰。
儿童相见不相识，
笑问客从何处来。

Home-Coming (I)

He Zhizhang

I left home young and not till old do I come back,
Unchanged my accent, my hair no longer black.
The children whom I meet do not know who am I,
"Where do you come from, sir?" they ask with beaming eye.

回乡偶书二首（其二）

贺知章

离别家乡岁月多，
近来人事半消磨。
唯有门前镜湖水，
春风不改旧时波。

Home-Coming (II)

He Zhizhang

Since I left my homeland so many years have passed;

So much has faded away and so little can last.

Only in Mirror Lake before my oldened door

The vernal wind still ripples waves now as before.

* *The old poet sighs for his changed look and the unchanged Mirror Lake.*

归　雁

钱　起

潇湘何事等闲回，
水碧沙明两岸苔。
二十五弦弹夜月，
不胜清怨却飞来。

To the North-flying Wild Geese[①]

Qian Qi

Why won't you stay on Southern River any more?

Why leave its water clear, sand bright and mossy shore?

You cannot bear the grief revealed in the moonlight

By the Princess' twenty-five strings, so you take flight.

* *The Princess refers to the daughter of Emperor Yao and wife to Emperor Shun who died on the Southern River, and the Princess played on the twenty-five strings to drown her grief.*

①本首诗与后面一首都是《归雁》，但翻译不同。本首采用翻译中"归化"的手法，解读原诗含义，提炼意境，将原诗幻化成读者更容易理解的目的语语言，同时保留了原诗的韵律之美；后面一首更多采用翻译中"异化"的手法，在充分尊重诗歌原作者的表达基础上，让意境隐藏蕴含在文字之下，表达更加含蓄，耐人寻味。两篇译文都不失为翻译的上乘之作。

归雁

钱起

潇湘何事等闲回？
水碧沙明两岸苔。
二十五弦弹夜月，
不胜清怨却飞来。

To the Returning Wild Geese

Qian Qi

Why will you stay on South River no more
With blue water, bright sand and mossy shore?
The moonbeams play on twenty-five sad strings.
Can you not bear the grief the zither brings?

* *The poet imagines the wild geese fly north for they cannot bear the grief of the princess who plays on a zither of twenty-five strings at the emperor's death by the riverside.*

登鹳雀楼

王之涣

白日依山尽，
黄河入海流。
欲穷千里目，
更上一层楼。

On the Stork Tower

Wang Zhihuan

The sun along the mountain bows;
The Yellow River seawards flows.
You will enjoy a grander sight
By climbing to a greater height.

凉州词

王之涣

黄河远上白云间，
一片孤城万仞山。
羌笛何须怨杨柳，
春风不度玉门关。

Out of the Great Wall

Wang Zhihuan

The Yellow River rises to the white cloud;

The lonely town is lost amid the mountains proud.

Why should the Mongol flute complain no willow grow?

Beyond the Gate of Jade no vernal wind will blow.

* *This quatrain describes a desolate scene out of the Gate of Jade, a part of the Great Wall.*

别董大

高 适

千里黄云白日曛，
北风吹雁雪纷纷。
莫愁前路无知己，
天下谁人不识君。

Farewell to a Lutist

Gao Shi

Yellow clouds spread for miles and miles have veiled the day;

The north wind blows down snow and wild geese fly away.

Fear not you've no admirers as you go along.

There is no connoisseur on earth but loves your song.

* *The poet believes that there is no connoisseur but loves the lutist's song.*

除夜作

高 适

旅馆寒灯独不眠，
客心何事转凄然。
故乡今夜思千里，
霜鬓明朝又一年。

Written on New Year's Eve

Gao Shi

Sleepless alone at an inn by cold lamplight,

Why should a roamer feel so sad and drear?

Thinking of my home far away tonight,

I'll have more frosty hair in the new year.

* *The poet is homesick on (lunar) Near Year's Eve when the family should get together.*

燕歌行

高　适

开元二十六年，客有从御史大夫张公出塞而还者，作《燕歌行》以示适，感征戍之事，因而和焉。

汉家烟尘在东北，
汉将辞家破残贼。
男儿本自重横行，
天子非常赐颜色。
摐金伐鼓下榆关，
旌旆逶迤碣石间。
校尉羽书飞瀚海，
单于猎火照狼山。
山川萧条极边土，
胡骑凭陵杂风雨。
战士军前半死生，
美人帐下犹歌舞。

Song of the Northern Frontier

Gao Shi

A cloud of smoke and dust spreads over northeast frontier;

To fight the remnant foe our generals leave the rear.

Brave men should go no manes where beneath the sky;

The emperor bestows on them his favor high.

To the beat of drums and gongs through Elm Pass they go;

Round Mount Stone Tablet flags serpentine row on row,

But urgent orders speed over the Sea of Sand:

Mount Wolf aflame with fires set by the Tartar band.

Both hills and streams are desolate on border plain;

The Tartar horsemen flurry like the wind and rain.

Half of our warriors lie killed on the battleground;

While pretty girls in camp still sing and dance their round.

大漠穷秋塞草腓，
孤城落日斗兵稀。
身当恩遇恒轻敌，
力尽关山未解围。
铁衣远戍辛勤久，
玉箸应啼别离后。
少妇城南欲断肠，
征人蓟北空回首。
边庭飘飖那可度，
绝域苍茫更何有。
杀气三时作阵云，
寒声一夜传刁斗。
相看白刃血纷纷，
死节从来岂顾勋。
君不见沙场征战苦，
至今犹忆李将军。

Grass withers in the desert as autumn is late;
At sunset few men guard the lonely city gate.
Imperial favor makes them hold the foemen light;
Their town is under siege, though they've fought with their might.
In coats of mail they've served so long on the frontiers;
Since they left home their wives have shed streams of impearled tears.
In southern towns the women weep with broken heart;
In vain their men look southward, still they're far apart.
The northern front at stake, how can they go away?
On border vast and desolate, how can they stay?
All day a cloud of slaughter mounts now and again;
All night the boom of gongs is heard to chill the plain.
Each sees the other's sword bloodstained in the hard strife.
Will they care for reward when they give up their life?
Do you not know the bitterness of fighting with the foe?
Can they forget General Li sharing their weal and woe?

* *The poet criticizes the proud generals defeated for they made light of the enemy, and glorifies General Li (2nd century BC) who shared weal and woe with his soldiers.*

别韦参军

高　适

二十解书剑，
西游长安城。
举头望君门，
屈指取公卿。
国风冲融迈三五，
朝廷礼乐弥寰宇。
白璧皆言赐近臣，
布衣不得干明主。
归来洛阳无负郭，
东过梁宋非吾土。
兔苑为农岁不登，

Farewell to Wei, a Military Officer

Gao Shi

I came at twenty with my sword and books
And visited the west capital town.
I gazed at your mansion with longing looks
And thought it easy to attain renown.
The emperor surpassed the ancient kings,
Music and rites were performed up and down.
He lavished on his favorites jade rings,
But unknown talents can't come near the Crown.
What could I do but come back to my land?
Going east, I could not do what I wish.
I cannot earn a living by the hand,

雁池垂钓心长苦。
世人遇我同众人，
唯君于我最相亲。
且喜百年有交态，
未尝一日辞家贫。
弹棋击筑白日晚，
纵酒高歌杨柳春。
欢娱未尽分散去，
使我惆怅惊心神。
丈夫不作儿女别，
临歧涕泪沾衣巾。

Nor would I with a hook and line catch fish.

For the world, like a common people I appear;

But for you, I am dear and near as a compeer.

From year to year I thank you for your friendly way;

You've not refused a helping hand, not for a day.

We play chess and on lute till day fades into night;

We drink and croon in spring with willows in delight.

We'll separate when our joy has not come to an end.

How can my heart not be grieved to part with my friend?

But men at parting should not grieve as women do,

So shed no tears at crossroads when we bid adieu!

* *The poet is recommended by Wei to take part in the civil service examinations.*

送灵澈上人

刘长卿

苍苍竹林寺，
杳杳钟声晚。
荷笠带夕阳，
青山独归远。

Seeing off a Recluse

Liu Changqing

Green, green the temple amid bamboos,

Late, late bell rings out the evening.

Alone, he's lost in mountains blue,

With sunset his hat is carrying.

* *This quatrain is picturesque to show a recluse carrying sunset on his hat amid bamboos.*

送严士元

刘长卿

春风倚棹阖闾城，
水国春寒阴复晴。
细雨湿衣看不见，
闲花落地听无声。
日斜江上孤帆影，
草绿湖南万里情。
君去若逢相识问，
青袍今已误儒生。

Farewell to Yan Shiyuan

Liu Changqing

In vernal breeze outside town walls we stop our oar;
The cloudy weather turns fine on chilly river shore.
Our gowns are wet with drizzling rain although unseen;
The flowers fall at leisure unheard by ears keen.
Your lonely sail sets off at sunset on the stream;
The grass will green for miles the southern shore in dream.
If you meet with some friends who inquire after me,
Tell them the blue-gowned petty official's carefree.

* *The poet describes the scenes and discloses his mind to his friend.*

行军九日思长安故园

岑 参

强欲登高去，
无人送酒来。
遥怜故园菊，
应傍战场开。

Thinking of Home While Marching on Mountain-climbing Day

Cen Shen

Up the mountain I'd force myself to go,

But nobody would bring me wine around.

Chrysanthemums of my homeland should blow

To beautify the far-off battleground.

* *The poet would drink and enjoy chrysanthemums at home on Mountain-climbing Day.*

逢入京使

岑　参

故园东望路漫漫，
双袖龙钟泪不干。
马上相逢无纸笔，
凭君传语报平安。

On Meeting a Messenger Going to the Capital

Cen Shen

I look eastward, long, long my homeward way appears;

My old arms tremble and my sleeves are wet with tears.

Meeting you on horseback, with what brush can I write?

I can but ask you to tell my kin I'm all right.

* *The quatrain is a short message the poet asks the messenger to send home.*

送李副使赴碛西官军

岑参

火山六月应更热，
赤亭道口行人绝。
知君惯度祁连城，
岂能愁见轮台月。
脱鞍暂入酒家垆，
送君万里西击胡。
功名只向马上取，
真是英雄一丈夫。

Seeing General Li Off to the West

Cen Shen

Fiery Mountain in sixth moon hotter than before,
No people pass by Red Pavilion any more.
I know you're used to hardship on the west frontier;
Oh, could the moon over Wheel Tower make you drear?
Unsaddle your horse, drink and drown in wine your woe;
I'll see you go for miles and miles to beat the foe.
You will win rank and fame only on battle steed;
A real hero must have done heroic deed.

轮台歌奉送封大夫出师西征

岑参

轮台城头夜吹角，
轮台城北旄头落。
羽书昨夜过渠黎，
单于已在金山西。
戍楼西望烟尘黑，
汉兵屯在轮台北。
上将拥旄西出征，
平明吹笛大军行。
四边伐鼓雪海涌，
三军大呼阴山动。

Song of Wheel Tower in Farewell to General Feng on His Western Expedition

Cen Shen

At night the horn blows on Wheel Tower walls;
The Tartar Star north of Wheel Tower falls.
Feathered dispatch passed southeast of the town:
West of Mount Gold Tartar chiefs settled down.
From the lookout we see dust raised by horses;
North of Wheel Tower camp the royal forces.
Our general with flags will westwards go;
At dawn the army march when bugles blow.
Frozen waves surge when drums are booming out;
The Shady Mountain trembles at soldiers' shout.

虏塞兵气连云屯，
战场白骨缠草根。
剑河风急雪片阔，
沙口石冻马蹄脱。
亚相勤王甘苦辛，
誓将报主静边尘。
古来青史谁不见，
今见功名胜古人。

Over Tartar forts clouds shiver at war cry;

On battleground white bones with grass roots lie.

Over Sword Stream swirling wind drives clouds on flake;

On frozen stone at Sand Mouth horsehoofs break.

Deputy commander, you bear all pain;

You swear to pacify, the border plain.

Have you not read the history of yore?

We love not ancients less, but moderns more.

* *The poet imagines a battle between the Tartar forces and the royal army led by General Feng.*

白雪歌送武判官归京

岑 参

北风卷地白草折，
胡天八月即飞雪。
忽如一夜春风来，
千树万树梨花开。
散入珠帘湿罗幕，
狐裘不暖锦衾薄。
将军角弓不得控，
都护铁衣冷难着。
瀚海阑干百丈冰，
愁云惨淡万里凝。
中军置酒饮归客，

Song of White Snow in Farewell to Secretary Wu Going Back to the Capital

Cen Shen

Snapping the pallid grass, the northern wind whirls low;

In the eighth moon the Tartar sky is filled with snow.

As if the vernal breeze had come back overnight,

Adorning thousands of pear trees with blossoms white.

Flakes enter pearled blinds and wet the silken screen;

No furs of fox can warm us nor brocade quilts green.

The general cannot draw his rigid bow with ease;

E'en the commissioner in coat of mail would freeze.

A thousand feet o'er cracked wilderness ice piles,

And gloomy clouds hang sad and drear for miles and miles.

We drink in headquarters to our guest homeward bound;

胡琴琵琶与羌笛。
纷纷暮雪下辕门，
风掣红旗冻不翻。
轮台东门送君去，
去时雪满天山路。
山回路转不见君，
雪上空留马行处。

With Tartar lutes, pipas and pipes the camps resound.

Snow in huge flakes at dusk falls heavy on camp gate;

The frozen red flag in the wind won't undulate.

At eastern gate of Wheel Tower we bid goodbye

On the snow-covered road to Heaven's Mountain high.

I watch his horse go past a bend and, lost to sight,

His track will soon be buried up by snow in flight.

* *The poet describes the biting cold on the frontier.*

走马川行奉送封大夫出师西征

岑 参

君不见走马川、
雪海边，
平沙莽莽黄入天。
轮台九月风夜吼，
一川碎石大如斗，
随风满地石乱走。
匈奴草黄马正肥，
金山西见烟尘飞，
汉家大将西出师。
将军金甲夜不脱，
半夜军行戈相拨，

Song of the Running Horse River in Farewell to General Feng on His Western Expedition

Cen Shen

Do you not see the Running Horse River flow
Along the sea of snow
And the sand that's yellowed sky and earth high and low?
In the ninth moon at Wheel Tower winds howl at night;
The river fills with boulders fallen from the height;
With howling winds they run riot as if in flight.
When grass turns yellow and plump Hunnish horses neigh,
West of Mount Gold dusts rise, the foe in proud array.
Our general leads his army on his westward way.
He keeps his iron armor on the whole night long,
Spears clang at midnight when his army march along,

风头如刀面如割。
马毛带雪汗气蒸，
五花连钱旋作冰，
幕中草檄砚水凝。
虏骑闻之应胆慑，
料知短兵不敢接，
车师西门伫献捷。

Their faces cut by winds that blow so sharp and strong.
Their sweat and snow turn into steam on horse's mane,
Which soon on horse's back turns into ice again;
Ink freezes when challenge's written before campaign.
On hearing this, the foe with fear should palpitate.
Dare they cross swords with our brave men in iron plate?
We'll wait for news of victory at the western gate.

* *This song glorifies General Feng in praise of his heroism against wind and snow.*

凉州馆中与诸判官夜集

岑参

弯弯月出挂城头，
城头月出照凉州。
凉州七里十万家，
胡人半解弹琵琶。
琵琶一曲肠堪断，
风萧萧兮夜漫漫。
河西幕中多故人，
故人别来三五春。
花门楼前见秋草，
岂能贫贱相看老。
一生大笑能几回，
斗酒相逢须醉倒。

Drinking with Friends at Night in Liangzhou

Cen Shen

The crescent moon rises and hangs on city wall;
The rising moon on city wall shines over all.
There're a thousand homes in seven districts on frontier;
Half of the Tartars play pipa for us to hear.
The heart would be broken to hear the pipa song,
When the wind sheds leaves in showers and night is long.
West of the River I have so many compeers;
Many friends are separated from me for many years.
Before the flowery gate we see autumn grass.
Could we bear to see friends grow old like it? Alas!
How many times can we laugh in a life so fleet?
So let us drink our fill till drunken, now we meet!

* *This poem sings of friendship and wine-drinking.*

黄鹤楼

崔　颢

昔人已乘黄鹤去，
此地空余黄鹤楼。
黄鹤一去不复返，
白云千载空悠悠。
晴川历历汉阳树，
芳草萋萋鹦鹉洲。
日暮乡关何处是？
烟波江上使人愁。

Yellow Crane Tower

Cui Hao

The sage on yellow crane was gone amid clouds white.

To what avail is Yellow Crane Tower left here?

Once gone, the yellow crane will not on earth alight;

Only white clouds still float in vain from year to year.

By sunlit river trees can be counted one by one;

On Parrot Islet sweet green grass grows fast and thick.

Where is my native land beyond the setting sun?

The mist-veiled waves of River Han makes me homesick.

* *The legend goes that the Yellow Crane Tower was built in memory of a sage who, riding on a yellow crane, flew to Heaven and became an immortal.*

三

留得枯荷听雨声

·中晚唐·

自初唐、盛唐以降，大唐滑向中晚期。也许是累了倦了，历史大潮不再能够裹挟一切。诗人依旧登临送目，依旧去国远游，依旧一袭薄衫，但却不再那么愤世傲俗，不再那么胸怀天下，不再那么豪气干云。他们的诗句变得更加纯粹、更加精致。“一生空吟诗”“两句三年得”，做诗似乎成了他们的主业而非宦而不达的排遣。当然，做为传统文人，修齐治平永远是他们的追求，也是他们永远的痛，尤其在帝国走向衰微之时。文人走向“躲进小楼成一统”“隔江犹唱后庭花”的例子并不少见，当然也少不了“我以我血荐轩辕”的真正的勇士，少不了“势压东南百万州”的豪雄。只是“自古美人如名将，不许人间见白头”。美人如此，名将如此，煌煌帝国更是如此——“故国不堪回首月明中”可为注脚。这就不难理解中晚唐诗歌“寒瘦奇绝”中有着令人心痛的美。江河日下，诗人还能做些什么呢？于是他们同帝国一起走向残星数点的天边，他们的背影孑遗孤寒，嘴里却依旧是阵阵苦吟。行将落幕，只有“留得枯荷听雨声”罢了。

枫桥夜泊

张　继

月落乌啼霜满天，
江枫渔火对愁眠。
姑苏城外寒山寺，
夜半钟声到客船。

Mooring by Maple Bridge at Night

Zhang Ji

The crows at moonset cry, streaking the frosty sky;

Facing dim fishing boats neath maples, sad I lie.

Beyond the city wall, from Temple of Cold Hill

Bells break the ship-borne roamer's dream in midnight still.

* *This quatrain gives a gloomy picture of a roamer dreaming of home in a dimly-lit boat. What he sees is moonset, frosty sky, dimly-lit fishing boats, dark maple trees. What he hears is crows' caw and temple bells. The outer gloom intensifies his inner gloom.*

江南行

张　潮

茨菰叶烂别西湾，
莲子花开不见还。
妾梦不离江上水，
人传郎在凤凰山。

Song of the Southern Rivershore

Zhang Chao

When leaves fell in decay, you left the western bay,

But you have not come back now lotus blossoms sway.

My dream oft lingers on the stream or by the fountain,

But you are said to be far away in the mountain.

* *A merchant's wife on the Southern Rivershore longs for her husband who left her in autumn but has not come back in summer. She compares her longing to the long river, but her husband is far away in the far-off mountain.*

题雍川山水

戴叔伦

松下茅亭五月凉，
汀沙云树晚苍苍。
行人无限秋风思，
隔水青山似故乡。

A Scenery like His Homeland

Dai Shulun

Summer is cool beneath thatched roof under the pine,
Clouds cast a gloom over the trees and the sand fine.
In autumn breeze the roamer will sink in a dream.
How like his homeland look hills beyond the stream!

* *The poet does not describe the scenery so much as his own feeling.*

兰溪棹歌

戴叔伦

凉月如眉挂柳湾，
越中山色镜中看。
兰溪三日桃花雨，
半夜鲤鱼来上滩。

A Fisherman's Song on the Orchid Stream

Dai Shulun

The eyebrow-like cool moon hangs over Willow Bay,

The southern mountains seem in the mirror to sway.

Three days rain's fallen with peach petals on the stream;

At midnight on the beach leap the fish, carp and bream.

* *This short song describes the beauty of the Orchid Stream and the joy of a fisherman.*

江南曲

李　益

嫁得瞿塘贾，
朝朝误妾期。
早知潮有信，
嫁与弄潮儿。

A Southern Song

Li Yi

Since I became a merchant's wife,

I've in his absence passed my life.

A sailor comes home with the tide,

I should have been a sailor's bride.

* *This song reveals the regret of a merchant's wife whose husband has not kept his promise to come home in due time as a sailor who would come back with the tide.*

写情

李益

水纹珍簟思悠悠，
千里佳期一夕休。
从此无心爱良夜，
任他明月下西楼。

A Date

Li Yi

On bamboo mat I long for you without a break,

Coming from afar, you don't keep the date you make.

From now on, I won't care for any lovely night;

In vain on the west tower may the moon shine bright.

* *The poet describes a woman waiting for her lover who has not kept his promise.*

汴河曲

李　益

汴水东流无限春，
隋家宫阙已成尘。
行人莫上长堤望，
风起杨花愁杀人。

Song of River Bian

Li Yi

The River Bian flows eastward, overwhelmed with spring;

To dust have gone ruined palaces and their king.

Don't gaze afar from the long bank of willow trees!

The willow down will grieve your heart when blows the breeze.

* *The River Bian refers to the canal built by the pleasure-making Emperor Yang of the Sui Dynasty (581—618), which was soon overthrown by the up-rising armies.*

夜上受降城闻笛

李　益

回乐峰前沙似雪，
受降城外月如霜。
不知何处吹芦管，
一夜征人尽望乡。

On Hearing a Flute at Night atop the Victor's Wall

Li Yi

Before the beacon tower sand looks white as snow;

Beyond the Victor's Wall like frost cold moonbeams flow.

None knows from where a flute blows a nostalgic song,

All warriors lie awake homesick the whole night long.

* *Hearing a flute song, the warriors on the frontier are drowned in homesickness.*

隋宫燕

李 益

燕语如伤旧国春，
宫花旋落已成尘。
自从一闭风光后，
几度飞来不见人。

Swallows in the Ruined Palace

Li Yi

The swallows' twitter seems to grieve over the lost spring;
To dust have returned palace flowers on the wing.
Since the overthrown dynasty closed its splendid scene,
They have come many times but nobody is seen.

* *The poet imagines swallows grieve over the ruined palace of the overthrown dynasty.*

喜见外弟又言别

李　益

十年离乱后，
长大一相逢。
问姓惊初见，
称名忆旧容。
别来沧海事，
语罢暮天钟。
明日巴陵道，
秋山又几重。

Meeting and Parting with My Cousin

Li Yi

We parted young for ten long years;
Not till grown up do we meet again.
At first I think a stranger appears;
Your name reminds me of your face then.
We talk of changes night and day
Until we hear the evening bell.
Tomorrow you'll go southward way
Over autumn hills, O farewell!

* *The poet parted with his young cousin in time of war and met with him ten years later when they were grown up.*

古别离

孟　郊

欲别牵郎衣，
“郎今到何处？
不恨归来迟，
莫向临邛去！”

Leave Me Not

Meng Jiao

I hold your robe lest you should go.
"Where are you going, dear, today?
Your late return brings me less woe
Than your heart being stolen away."

* *This quatrain reveals a wife's fear of being deserted.*

登科后

孟 郊

昔日龌龊不足夸，
今朝放荡思无涯。
春风得意马蹄疾，
一日看尽长安花。

Successful at the Civil Service Examinations

Meng Jiao

Gone are all my past woes! What more have I to say?
My body and my mind enjoy their fill today.
Successful, faster runs my horse in vernal breeze;
I've seen within one day all flowers on the trees.

* *This is the most balanced verse in Tang poetry.*

游子吟

孟郊

慈母手中线，
游子身上衣。
临行密密缝，
意恐迟迟归。
谁言寸草心，
报得三春晖。

Song of the Parting Son

Meng Jiao

From the threads a mother's hand weaves,
A gown for parting son is made.
Sown stitch by stitch before he leaves,
For fear his return be delayed.
Such kindness as young grass receives
From the warm sun can't be repaid.

* *This is a well-known song showing the mother's love for her son.*

古怨别

孟郊

飒飒秋风生，
愁人怨离别。
含情两相向，
欲语气先咽。
心曲千万端，
悲来却难说。
别后唯所思，
天涯共明月。

Complaint of Parting

Meng Jiao

The soughing autumn wind is blowing;

Grieved, I complain my man is going.

We face each other eye to eye;

Before I speak, I sob and sigh.

My heart is like a winding stream,

How can I tell my dreary dream?

When I miss him after we part,

We can but share moonlight apart.

* *This poem describes a woman complaining of the separation from her lord.*

巫山曲

孟　郊

巴江上峡重复重，
阳台碧峭十二峰。
荆王猎时逢暮雨，
夜卧高丘梦神女。
轻红流烟湿艳姿，
行云飞去明星稀。
目极魂断望不见，
猿啼三声泪滴衣。

Song of the Mountain Goddess

Meng Jiao

Going upstream, I see mountain on mountain high;
The twelve green peaks with Sunny Terrace scrape the sky.
The king in hunting caught by sudden evening shower
Slept there and dreamed of the Goddess in Sunny Bower.
To her charm added the mist-veiled rainbow dress bright;
Away she flew with faded stars and clouds in flight.
However far I stretch my eyes, she can't be found;
Hearing the monkey's wail, in longing tears I'm drowned.

* *The legend goes that King Xiang of Chu dreamed of the Mountain Goddess and made love with her in the Sunny Bower, and she would come in morning cloud and go away in evening shower. The poet sees the Peak of Goddess and writes this poem.*

湘江曲

张 籍

湘水无潮秋水阔，
湘中月落行人发。
送人发，送人归，
白蘋茫茫鹧鸪飞。

Song on River Xiang

Zhang Ji

The River Xiang unruffled in autumn looks wide;

The wayfarer at moonset leaves the riverside.

We see wayfarers come, we see wayfarers go.

Over white duckweed partridges fly to and fro.

* *In this quatrain the wayfarers are compared to partridges flying to and fro.*

春　雪

韩　愈

新年都未有芳华，
二月初惊见草芽。
白雪却嫌春色晚，
故穿庭树作飞花。

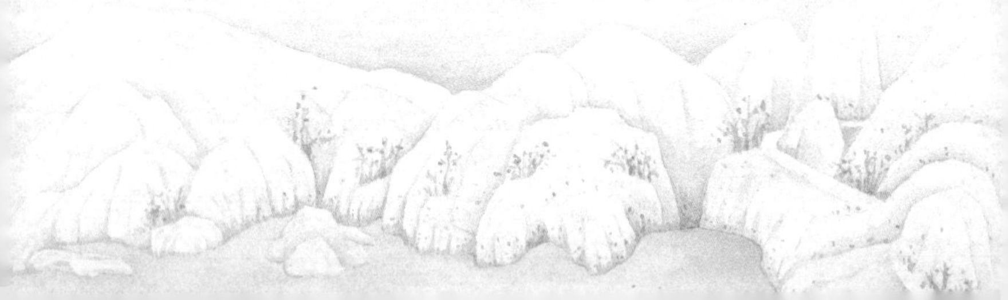

Spring Snow

Han Yu

On vernal day no flowers were in bloom, alas!

In second moon I'm glad to see the budding grass.

But white snow dislikes the late coming vernal breeze,

It plays the parting flowers flying through the trees.

* *Spring snow is compared to flying flowers in this quatrain.*

晚 春

韩 愈

草树知春不久归，
百般红紫斗芳菲。
杨花榆荚无才思，
唯解漫天作雪飞。

Late Spring

Han Yu

The trees and grass know that soon spring will go away;

Of red blooms and green leaves they make gorgeous display.

But willow catkins and elm pods are so unwise,

They wish to be flying snow darkening the skies.

* *Flying flowers are compared to spring snow in this quatrain.*

左迁至蓝关示侄孙湘

韩　愈

一封朝奏九重天，
夕贬潮州路八千。
欲为圣明除弊事，
肯将衰朽惜残年。
云横秦岭家何在，
雪拥蓝关马不前。
知汝远来应有意，
好收吾骨瘴江边。

Written for My Grandnephew at the Blue Pass

Han Yu

To the Celestial Court a proposal was made,

And I am banished eight thousand li away.

To undo the misdeeds I would have given aid,

Dare I have spared myself with powers in decay?

The Ridge veiled in barred clouds, where can my home be seen?

The Blue Pass clad in snow, my horse won't forward go.

You have come from afar and I know what you mean:

Not to leave my bones there where miasmic waves flow.

* *The old poet was banished for his anti-Buddhist proposal.*

再游玄都观

刘禹锡

百亩庭中半是苔，
桃花净尽菜花开。
种桃道士归何处，
前度刘郎今又来。

The Taoist Temple Revisited

Liu Yuxi

In half of the wide courtyard only mosses grow;

Peach blossoms all fallen, only rape-flowers blow.

Where is the Taoist planting peach trees in this place?

I come after I fell again into disgrace.

* *In 828 the poet came again to the Taoist temple after his second banishment in 815.*

元和十年自朗州召至京师戏赠看花诸君子

刘禹锡

紫陌红尘拂面来，
无人不道看花回。
玄都观里桃千树，
尽是刘郎去后栽。

The Flower-admirers

Liu Yuxi

Dust raised by cabs on grassy lane caresses my face;
No flower-admirers but follow the cabs' trace.
Thousands of peach trees in the Taoist temple's place
Are all planted after I fell into disgrace.

* *In 815 the poet lamented over his banishment from the capital in 805 with the result that he could not admire the peach flowers in the Taoist temple.*

石头城

刘禹锡

山围故国周遭在，
潮打空城寂寞回。
淮水东边旧时月，
夜深还过女墙来。

The Town of Stone

Liu Yuxi

The changeless hills round ancient capital still stand;
Waves beating on ruined walls, unheeded, roll away.
The moon which shone by riverside on flourished land
Still shines at dead of night over ruined town today.

* *The town of stone refers to Jinling capital of six dynasties* (*222—580*).

乌衣巷

刘禹锡

朱雀桥边野草花，
乌衣巷口夕阳斜。
旧时王谢堂前燕，
飞入寻常百姓家。

The Street of Mansions

Liu Yuxi

Beside the Bridge of Birds rank grasses overgrow;

Over the Street of Mansions the setting sun hangs low.

Swallows which skimmed by painted eaves in days gone by,

Are dipping now in homes where humble people occupy.

* *The Street of Mansions were inhabited by the noble and the rich during the Jin Dynasty (265—420).*

杨柳枝词（其一）

刘禹锡

塞北梅花羌笛吹，
淮南桂树小山词。
请君莫奏前朝曲，
听唱新翻杨柳枝。

Willow Branch Songs (I)

Liu Yuxi

The flute played on "Mume Blossoms" on Northern Frontier,
"The Laurel Branch" to Southern River shore was dear.
They were sung in the former dynasties for long.
Now listen to my newly composed "Willow Song" .

竹枝词二首（其一）

刘禹锡

杨柳青青江水平，
闻郎江上唱歌声。
东边日出西边雨，
道是无晴却有晴。

Bamboo Branch Songs (I)

Liu Yuxi

Between the green willows the river flows along;
My gallant in a boat is heard to sing a song.
The west is veiled in rain, the east enjoys sunshine,
My gallant is as deep in love as the day is fine.

竹枝词九首（其二）

刘禹锡

山桃红花满上头，
蜀江春水拍山流。
花红易衰似郎意，
水流无限似侬愁。

Bamboo Branch Songs (II)

Liu Yuxi

The mountain's red with peach blossoms above;
The shore is washed by spring waves below.
Red blossoms fade fast as my gallant's love;
The river like my sorrow will ever flow.

* *These two quatrains describe a woman's complaint of her gallant.*

竹枝词九首（其七）

刘禹锡

瞿塘嘈嘈十二滩，
此中道路古来难。
长恨人心不如水，
等闲平地起波澜。

Bamboo Branch Songs (VII)

Liu Yuxi

From beach to beach the torrent splashes down its way;

It's hard to sail in the Three Gorges since olden day.

But human heart is more dangerous than a whirlpool;

You may be drowned in it though it seems calm and cool.

* *The poet compares human heart to a dangerous whirlpool.*

蜀先主庙

刘禹锡

天下英雄气，
千秋尚凛然。
势分三足鼎，
业复五铢钱。
得相能开国，
生儿不象贤。
凄凉蜀故妓，
来舞魏宫前。

Temple of the King of Shu

Liu Yuxi

Your heroism under the sky
From year to year spread far and nigh.
Like tripod did three kingdoms reign;
Old royal coins were used again.
Your premier struck your kingdom's root;
But your son did not follow suit.
Even Western dancers felt sad
To make Northern conquerors glad.

* *The Han Empire was divided into three kingdoms: Wei in the north, Wu in the east and Shu in the west where coins of the Han Dynasty were used. After the death of the King of Shu, his son surrendered to the King of Wei and enjoyed the Western dance as if he were not a captive of the Northern Kingdom, and even dancers of Shu were grieved.*

金陵怀古

刘禹锡

潮满冶城渚，
日斜征虏亭。
蔡洲新草绿，
幕府旧烟青。
兴废由人事，
山川空地形。
后庭花一曲，
幽怨不堪听。

Memories at Jinling

Liu Yuxi

The tide overwhelms the forge's site,

The tower drowned in slanting sunlight.

The islet covered with grass green,

And hills are veiled by a smoke screen.

Man decides a state's rise and fall,

Hills and streams can do nothing at all.

O hear the captive ruler's song!

How can you bear his grief for long?

* *Jinling was the capital of six dynasties (222—580). The last ruler fond of pleasure-making became a captive and the place where weapons were forged was overwhelmed by the tide.*

再授连州至衡阳酬柳柳州赠别

刘禹锡

去国十年同赴召，
渡湘千里又分歧。
重临事异黄丞相，
三黜名惭柳士师。
归目并随回雁尽，
愁肠正遇断猿时。
桂江东过连山下，
相望长吟有所思。

Farewell to Liu Zongyuan in Exile

Liu Yuxi

Recalled together after an exile of ten years,
Again we're banished for long miles and say adieu.
We reappear but unlike our noble compeers;
Thrice in exile I feel I'm unworthy of you.
We watch returning wild geese till they're out of sight;
We're sad to hear the monkey wail with broken heart.
The Western River flows far from the Southern height.
Longing for each other, can we be kept apart?

* *The poet was banished to the south and his friend to the west for ten years, both were recalled and again banished together, but the poet said he was unworthy of his friend for he was not so straightforward.*

始闻秋风

刘禹锡

昔看黄菊与君别，
今听玄蝉我却回。
五夜飕飗枕前觉，
一年颜状镜中来。
马思边草拳毛动，
雕眄青云睡眼开。
天地肃清堪四望，
为君扶病上高台。

Ode to the Autumn Breeze

Liu Yuxi

Gone with yellow chrysanthemums last year,
You come back when cicada's song I hear.
Your soughing wakes me from dreams at midnight,
A year's wrinkles are seen in mirror bright.
Steeds missing frontier grass with bristles rise;
Eagles longing for clouds open sleepy eyes.
I'll gaze my fill into the boundless sky;
Though ill, for you I'll mount the tower high.

* *The poet shows his spirit to go higher and see farther in the melancholy season.*

西塞山怀古

刘禹锡

王濬楼船下益州，
金陵王气黯然收。
千寻铁锁沉江底，
一片降幡出石头。
人世几回伤往事，
山形依旧枕寒流。
今逢四海为家日，
故垒萧萧芦荻秋。

Mount Western Fort

Liu Yuxi

The Northern galleys went along the stream;
The Eastern kingdom vanished like a dream.
The iron chains could not bar the barges light;
The Eastern king surrendered with flags white.
How many times have we grieved over the past!
Mountains commanding the river still last.
We're glad the world is unified today,
But the fort shivers to see the reed sway.

* *The King of Wu in the East tried to bar the river with iron chains, but the galleys of Jin in the North broke through and captured the King of Wu in 280. The fort shivers for it has witnessed the rise and fall of kingdoms.*

暮江吟

白居易

一道残阳铺水中，
半江瑟瑟半江红。
可怜九月初三夜，
露似真珠月似弓。

Sunset and Moonrise on the River

Bai Juyi

The departing sunbeams pave a way on the river;

Half of its waves turn red and the other half shiver.

How I love the third night of the ninth moon aglow!

The dewdrops look like pearls, the crescent like a bow.

* *This quatrain describes the poet's love of the beautiful river at sunset and at moonrise.*

杨柳枝词

白居易

一树春风千万枝，
嫩于金色软于丝。
永丰西角荒园里，
尽日无人属阿谁？

Song of Willow Branch

Bai Juyi

A tree of million branches sways in breeze of spring,
More tender, more soft than golden silk string by string.
But in west corner of a garden in decay,
Who would come to admire its beauty all the day?

* *This quatrain reveals the poet's sympathy for a willow tree in a decayed garden.*

惜牡丹花二首（其一）

白居易

惆怅阶前红牡丹，
晚来唯有两枝残。
明朝风起应吹尽，
夜惜衰红把火看。

The Last Look at the Peonies at Night (I)

Bai Juyi

I'm saddened by the courtyard peonies brilliant red,
At dusk only two of them are left on their bed.
I am afraid they can't survive the morning blast,
By lantern light I take a look at the long, long last.

* *This quatrain reveals the poet's love for the last peonies in his courtyard.*

大林寺桃花

白居易

人间四月芳菲尽，
山寺桃花始盛开。
长恨春归无觅处，
不知转入此中来。

Peach Blossoms in the Temple of Great Forest

Bai Juyi

All flowers in late spring have fallen far and wide,

But peach blossoms are full-blown on this mountainside.

I oft regret spring's gone without leaving its trace;

I do not know it's come up to adorn this place.

* *The poet expresses his joy at seeing peach blossoms in Mount Lu when other flowers are all fallen in late spring.*

白云泉

白居易

天平山上白云泉，
云自无心水自闲。
何必奔冲山下去，
更添波浪向人间！

White Cloud Fountain

Bai Juyi

Behold the White Cloud Fountain on the sky-blue Mountain!

White clouds enjoy pleasure while water enjoys leisure.

Why should the torrent dash down from the mountain high

And overflow the human world with waves far and nigh?

* *This quatrain shows the poet's love of freedom.*

舟中读元九诗

白居易

把君诗卷灯前读，
诗尽灯残天未明。
眼痛灭灯犹暗坐，
逆风吹浪打船声。

Reading Yuan Zhen's Poems in a Boat

Bai Juyi

I read your book of poetry by the lamplight,

And finish it when oil burns low at dead of night.

Eyes sore, I blow the light out and sit in the dark;

The waves brought up by adverse wind beat on the bark.

* *The poet and his friend are in exile, so he feels waves rise in his heart as on the river.*

邯郸冬至夜思家

白居易

邯郸驿里逢冬至，
抱膝灯前影伴身。
想得家中夜深坐，
还应说着远行人。

Thinking of Home on Winter Solstice Night at Handan

Bai Juyi

At roadside inn I pass the Winter Solstice Day,

Clasping my knees, with my shadow in company.

I think, till dead of night my family would stay,

And talk about the poor lonely wayfaring me.

* *While young, the poet thought of home at a lonely inn on Winter Solstice Day, which was as important as New Year's Day during the Tang Dynasty.*

望驿台

白居易

靖安宅里当窗柳，
望驿台前扑地花。
两处春光同日尽，
居人思客客思家。

For Roaming Yuan Zhen

Bai Juyi

Your wife gazes at yellowing willows at home;
You on flowers falling on the ground while you roam.
Spring comes to end in two places on the same day;
You think of home and she of you far, far away.

* *Yuan and his wife long for each other on seeing falling flowers and yellow leaves.*

赋得古原草送别

白居易

离离原上草，
一岁一枯荣。
野火烧不尽，
春风吹又生。
远芳侵古道，
晴翠接荒城。
又送王孙去，
萋萋满别情。

Grass on the Ancient Plain in Farewell to a Friend

Bai Juyi

Wild grasses spread over ancient plain;
With spring and fall they come and go.
Fire tries to burn them up in vain;
They rise again when spring winds blow.
Their fragrance overruns the way;
Their green invades the ruined town.
To see my friend going away,
My sorrow grows like grass overgrown.

* *The poet compares his friendship to the overgrown grass on the ancient plain.*

轻　肥

白居易

意气骄满路，
鞍马光照尘。
借问何为者？
人称是内臣。
朱绂皆大夫，
紫绶或将军。
夸赴军中宴，
走马去如云。
罇罍溢九酝，
水陆罗八珍。
果擘洞庭橘，

Sleek Horse and Light Furs

Bai Juyi

The road is overwhelmed with their pride,
Saddled steeds brighten the roadside.
How proud these officers appear
For they are eunuchs without fear!
They wear official tassels red
And violet ribbon round the head.
To feast in the army they're proud,
Their horses run as light as cloud.
They drink and eat, wine cup in hand,
Delicious food from sea and land.
The oranges come from the lakeside;

脍切天池鳞。
食饱心自若，
酒酣气益振。
是岁江南旱，
衢州人食人！

The fish from Heaven's Pool well fried.

Full fed, they set their heart at ease;

Drunken, they would do as they please.

This year in the south the drought rages;

Men eat human flesh like savages.

* *The poet criticizes the luxurious eunuchs and reminds them of the drought in the south.*

买　花

白居易

帝城春欲暮，
喧喧车马度。
共道牡丹时，
相随买花去。
贵贱无常价，
酬直看花数。
灼灼百朵红，
戋戋五束素。
上张幄幕庇，
旁织笆篱护。
水洒复泥封，
移来色如故。

Buying Flowers

Bai Juyi

The capital's in parting spring,
Steeds run and neigh and cab bells ring.
Peonies are at their best hours
And people rush to buy the flowers.
They do not care about the price,
Just count and buy those which seem nice.
For hundred blossoms dazzling red,
Twenty-five rolls of silk they spread.
Sheltered above by curtains wide,
Protected with fences by the side,
Roots sealed with mud, with water sprayed,
Removed, their beauty does not fade.

家家习为俗，
人人迷不悟。
有一田舍翁，
偶来买花处。
低头独长叹，
此叹无人谕。
一丛深色花，
十户中人赋！

Accustomed to this way for long,

No family e'er thinks it wrong.

What's the old peasant doing there?

Why should he come to Flower Fair?

Head bowed, he utters sigh on sigh

And nobody understands why.

A bunch of deep-red peonies

Costs taxes of ten families.

* *The poet compares the rich who buy flowers and the poor who pay taxes.*

钱塘湖春行

白居易

孤山寺北贾亭西，
水面初平云脚低。
几处早莺争暖树，
谁家新燕啄春泥。
乱花渐欲迷人眼，
浅草才能没马蹄。
最爱湖东行不足，
绿杨阴里白沙堤。

On Qiantang Lake in Spring

Bai Juyi

West of Jia Pavilion and north of Lonely Hill,
Water brims level with the bank and clouds hang low.
Disputing for sunny trees, early orioles trill;
Pecking vernal mud in, young swallows come and go.
A riot of blooms begins to dazzle the eye;
Amid short grass the horse hoofs can barely be seen.
I love best the east of the lake under the sky;
The bank paved with white sand is shaded by willows green.

* *Qiantang Lake is later known as the West Lake in Hangzhou, and Jia Pavilion and Lonely Hill are scenic spots to the east or south of the Lake.*

杭州春望

白居易

望海楼明照曙霞，
护江堤白踏晴沙。
涛声夜入伍员庙，
柳色春藏苏小家。
红袖织绫夸柿蒂，
青旗沽酒趁梨花。
谁开湖寺西南路，
草绿裙腰一道斜。

Spring View in Hangzhou

Bai Juyi

Viewed from the Seaside Tower morning clouds look bright;
Along the riverbank I tread on fine sand white.
The General's Temple hears roaring nocturnal tide;
Spring dwells in the Beauty's Bower green willow hide.
The red sleeves weave brocade broidered with flowers fine;
Blue streamers show amid pear blossoms a shop of wine.
Who opens a southwest lane to the temple scene?
It slants like a silk girdle around a skirt green.

* *The General refers to Wu Yuan whose wrath against the King of Chu seems to be heard in the roaring tide. The Beauty refers to Su Xiaoxiao who was buried in the West Lake.*

望月有感

白居易

自河南经乱，关内阻饥，兄弟离散，各在一处。因望月有感，聊书所怀，寄上浮梁大兄、于潜七兄、乌江十五兄，兼示符离及下邽弟妹。

时难年荒世业空，
弟兄羁旅各西东。
田园寥落干戈后，
骨肉流离道路中。
吊影分为千里雁，
辞根散作九秋蓬。
共看明月应垂泪，
一夜乡心五处同。

Feeling at the moon

Bai Juyi

Thinking of My Brothers and Sisters Scattered Here and There, I Write this Poem for Them by the Light of the Moon.

Hard times with famine spread ruins in our hometown;
My brothers go their way east or west, up and down.
Battles have left the fields and gardens desolate;
By roadside wander families wars separate.
Like far-off wild geese over lonely shadows we weep,
As scattered rootless tumbleweed in autumn deep.
We should shed yearning tears to view the moon apart;
Though in five places, we have the same homesick heart.

* *The poet shows his love for his brothers and sisters scattered in five places in wartime.*

琵琶行

白居易

浔阳江头夜送客，
枫叶荻花秋瑟瑟。
主人下马客在船，
举酒欲饮无管弦。
醉不成欢惨将别，
别时茫茫江浸月。
忽闻水上琵琶声，
主人忘归客不发。
寻声暗问弹者谁？
琵琶声停欲语迟。
移船相近邀相见，
添酒回灯重开宴。

Song of a Pipa Player

Bai Juyi

One night by riverside I bade a friend goodbye;
In maple leaves and rushes autumn seemed to sigh.
My friend and I dismounted and came into the boat;
We wished to drink but there was no music afloat.
Without flute songs we drank our cups with heavy hearts;
The moonbeams blended with water when we were to part.
Suddenly o'er the stream we heard a pipa sound;
I forgot to go home and the guest stood spell-bound.
We followed where the music led to find the player,
But heard the pipa stop and no music in the air.
We moved our boat towards the one whence came the strain,
Brought back the lamp, asked for more wine and drank again.

千呼万唤始出来，
犹抱琵琶半遮面。
转轴拨弦三两声，
未成曲调先有情。
弦弦掩抑声声思，
似诉平生不得志。
低眉信手续续弹，
说尽心中无限事。
轻拢慢捻抹复挑，
初为《霓裳》后《六幺》。
大弦嘈嘈如急雨，
小弦切切如私语。
嘈嘈切切错杂弹，
大珠小珠落玉盘。
间关莺语花底滑，
幽咽泉流水下滩。
水泉冷涩弦凝绝，

Repeatedly we called for the fair player till
She came, her face half hidden behind a pipa still.
She turned the pegs and tested twice or thrice each string;
Before a tune was played we heard her feelings sing.
Each string she plucked, each note she struck with pathos strong,
All seemed to say she'd missed her dreams all her life long.
Head bent, she played with unpremeditated art
On and on to pour out her overflowing heart.
She lightly plucked, slowly stroked and twanged loud
The song of "Green Waist" after that of "Rainbow Cloud" .
The thick strings loudly thrummed like the pattering rain;
The fine strings softly tinkled in a murmuring strain.
When mingling loud and soft notes were together played,
You heard large and small pearls cascade on plate of jade.
Now you heard orioles warble in flowery land,
Then a sobbing stream run along a beach of sand.
But the stream seemed so cold as to tighten the string;

凝绝不通声暂歇。
别有幽愁暗恨生，
此时无声胜有声。
银瓶乍破水浆迸，
铁骑突出刀枪鸣。
曲终收拨当心画，
四弦一声如裂帛。
东船西舫悄无言，
唯见江心秋月白。
沉吟放拨插弦中，
整顿衣裳起敛容。
自言本是京城女，
家在虾蟆陵下住。
十三学得琵琶成，
名属教坊第一部。
曲罢常教善才伏，
妆成每被秋娘妒。

From tightened strings no more sound could be heard to sing.
Still we heard hidden grief and vague regret concealed;
Then music expressed far less than silence revealed.
Suddenly we heard water burst a silver jar,
And the clash of spears and sabers come from afar.
She made a central sweep when the music was ending;
The four strings made one sound, as of silk one was rending.
Silence reigned left and right of the boat, east and west;
We saw but autumn moon white in the river's breast.
She slid the plectrum pensively between the strings,
Smoothed out her dress and rose with a composed mien.
"I spent," she said, "in the capital my early springs,
Where at the foot of Mount of Toads my home had been.
At thirteen I learned on the pipa how to play,
And my name was among the primas of the day.
I won my master's admiration for my skill;
My beauty was envied by songstresses fair still.

五陵年少争缠头，
一曲红绡不知数。
钿头银篦击节碎，
血色罗裙翻酒污。
今年欢笑复明年，
秋月春风等闲度。
弟走从军阿姨死，
暮去朝来颜色故。
门前冷落车马稀，
老大嫁作商人妇。
商人重利轻别离，
前月浮梁买茶去。
去来江口守空船，
绕船月明江水寒。
夜深忽梦少年事，
梦啼妆泪红阑干。
我闻琵琶已叹息，

The gallant young men vied to shower gifts on me;
One tune played, countless silk rolls were given with glee.
Beating time, I let silver comb and pin drop down,
And spilt-out wine oft stained my blood-red silken gown.
From year to year I laughed my joyous life away
On moonlit autumn night as windy vernal day.
My younger brother left for war, and died my maid;
Days passed, nights came, and my beauty began to fade.
Fewer and fewer were cabs and steeds at my door;
I married a smug merchant when my prime was o'er.
The merchant cared for money much more than for me.
One month ago he went away to purchase tea,
Leaving his lonely wife alone in empty boat;
Shrouded in moonlight, on the cold river I float.
Deep in the night I dreamed of happy bygone years,
And woke to find my rouged face crisscrossed with tears."
Listening to her sad music, I sighed with pain;

又闻此语重唧唧。
同是天涯沦落人，
相逢何必曾相识！
我从去年辞帝京，
谪居卧病浔阳城。
浔阳地僻无音乐，
终岁不闻丝竹声。
住近湓江地低湿，
黄芦苦竹绕宅生。
其间旦暮闻何物？
杜鹃啼血猿哀鸣。
春江花朝秋月夜，
往往取酒还独倾。
岂无山歌与村笛？
呕哑嘲哳难为听。
今夜闻君琵琶语，
如听仙乐耳暂明。

Hearing her story, I sighed again and again.

Both of us in misfortune go from shore to shore.

Meeting now, need we have known each other before?

"I was banished from the capital last year

To live degraded and ill in this city here.

The city's too remote to know melodious song,

So I have never heard music all the year long.

l dwell by riverbank on a low and damp ground

In a house with wild reeds and stunted bamboos around.

What is here to be heard from daybreak till nightfall

But gibbon's cry and cuckoo's homeward-going call?

By blooming riverside and under autumn moon

I've often taken wine up and drunk it alone.

Though I have mountain songs and village pipes to hear,

Yet they are crude and strident and grate on the ear.

Listening to you playing on pipa tonight,

With your music divine e'en my hearing seems bright.

莫辞更坐弹一曲，
为君翻作琵琶行。
感我此言良久立，
却坐促弦弦转急。
凄凄不似向前声，
满座重闻皆掩泣。
座中泣下谁最多，
江州司马青衫湿。

Will you sit down and play for us a tune once more?

I'll write for you an ode to the pipa I adore."

Touched by what I said, the player stood for long,

Then sat down, tore at strings and played another song.

So sad, so drear, so different, it moved us deep;

Those who heard it hid the face and began to weep.

Of all the company at table who wept most?

It was none other than the exiled blue-robed host.

* *This is one of the most popular songs of the Tang Dynasty in which the poet describes a musician and her music.*

与梦得沽酒闲饮且约后期

白居易

少时犹不忧生计，
老后谁能惜酒钱？
共把十千沽一斗，
相看七十欠三年。
闲征雅令穷经史，
醉听清吟胜管弦。
更待菊黄家酿熟，
共君一醉一陶然。

Drinking Together with Liu Yuxi

Bai Juyi

While young, I was not worded about livelihood.

Old now, how could I grudge money for buying wine?

Let's spend ten thousand coins for a jarful of drink good!

Looking in face, two years more we'll be sixty-nine.

We read and play the drinkers' wager game at leisure;

Drunk, we listen to verse better than music light.

When chrysanthemums yellow, may I have the pleasure

To invite you to drink my home-brew with delight?

* *The poet expresses his delight in drinking together with an old friend.*

上阳白发人

白居易

上阳人，上阳人，
红颜暗老白发新。
绿衣监使守宫门，
一闭上阳多少春。
玄宗末岁初选入，
入时十六今六十。
同时采择百余人，
零落年深残此身。
忆昔吞悲别亲族，
扶入车中不教哭。
皆云入内便承恩，
脸似芙蓉胸似玉。

The White-haired Palace Maid

Bai Juyi

The Shangyang Palace maid,
Her hair grows white, her rosy cheeks grow dark and fade.
The palace gate is guarded by eunuchs in green.
How many springs have passed, immured as she has been!
She was first chosen for the imperial household
At the age of sixteen; now she's sixty years old.
The hundred beauties brought in with her have all gone,
Flickering out through long years, leaving her alone.
She swallowed grief when she left home in days gone by,
Helped into the cab, she was forbidden to cry.
Once in the palace, she'd be favored, it was said;
Her face was fair as lotus, her bosom like jade.

未容君王得见面，
已被杨妃遥侧目。
妒令潜配上阳宫，
一生遂向空房宿。
宿空房，秋夜长，
夜长无寐天不明。
耿耿残灯背壁影，
萧萧暗雨打窗声。
春日迟，
日迟独坐天难暮；
宫莺百啭愁厌闻，
梁燕双栖老休妒。
莺归燕去长悄然，
春往秋来不记年。
唯向深宫望明月，
东西四五百回圆。
今日宫中年最老，

But to the emperor she could never come nigh,
For Lady Yang had cast on her a jealous eye.
She was consigned to Shangyang Palace full of gloom,
To pass her lonely days and nights in a bare room.
In empty chamber long seemed each autumnal night;
Sleepless in bed, it seemed she'd never see daylight.
Dim, dim the lamplight throws her shadow on the walls;
Shower by shower on her windows chill rain falls.
Spring days drag slow;
She sits alone to see light won't be dim and low.
She's tired to hear the palace orioles sing and sing,
Too old to envy pairs of swallows on the wing.
Silent, she sees the birds appear and disappear,
And counts nor springs nor autumns coming year by year.
Watching the moon o'er palace again and again,
Four hundred times and more she's seen it wax and wane.
Today the oldest honorable maid of all,

大家遥赐尚书号。
小头鞋履窄衣裳，
青黛点眉眉细长。
外人不见见应笑，
天宝末年时世妆。
上阳人，苦最多：
少亦苦，老亦苦，
少苦老苦两如何？
君不见昔时吕向《美人赋》，
又不见今日上阳宫人白发歌。

She is entitled Secretary of Palace Hall.

Her gown is tightly fitted, her shoes like pointed prows;

With dark green pencil she draws long, long slender brows.

Seeing her, outsiders would even laugh with tears;

Her old-fashioned dress has been out of date for years.

The Shangyang maid, to suffer is her fate, all told;

She suffered while still young; she suffers now she's old.

Do you not know a satire spread in days gone by?

Today for white-haired Shangyang Palace maid we'll sigh.

* *The poet pities the place maid who lived the palace from sixteen to sixty without even seeing the emperor's face.*

卖炭翁

白居易

卖炭翁，
伐薪烧炭南山中。
满面尘灰烟火色，
两鬓苍苍十指黑。
卖炭得钱何所营？
身上衣裳口中食。
可怜身上衣正单，
心忧炭贱愿天寒。
夜来城外一尺雪，
晓驾炭车辗冰辙。
牛困人饥日已高，
市南门外泥中歇。

The Old Charcoal Seller

Bai Juyi

What does the old man fare?

He cuts the wood in southern hill and fires his ware.

His face is grimed with smoke and streaked with ash and dust,

His temples grizzled and his fingers all turned black.

The money earned by selling charcoal is not just

Enough for food for his mouth and clothing for his back.

Though his coat is thin, he hopes winter will set in,

For cold weather will keep up the charcoals good price.

At night a foot of snow falls outside city walls;

At dawn his charcoal cart crushes ruts in the ice.

The sun is high, the ox tired out and hungry he;

Outside the southern gate in snow and slush they rest.

翩翩两骑来是谁？
黄衣使者白衫儿。
手把文书口称敕，
回车叱牛牵向北。
一车炭，千余斤，
宫使驱将惜不得。
半匹红纱一丈绫，
系向牛头充炭直。

Two riders canter up. Alas! Who can they be?

Two palace heralds in the yellow jackets dressed.

Decree in hand, which is imperial order, one says;

They turn the cart about and at the ox they shout.

A cartload of charcoal a thousand catties weighs;

They drive the cart away. What dare the old man say?

Ten feet of silk and twenty feet of gauze deep red,

That is the payment they fasten to the ox's head.

* *The poet sympathizes with the old charcoal seller in poverty and in misery.*

长恨歌

白居易

汉皇重色思倾国，
御宇多年求不得。
杨家有女初长成，
养在深闺人未识。
天生丽质难自弃，
一朝选在君王侧。
回眸一笑百媚生，
六宫粉黛无颜色。
春寒赐浴华清池，
温泉水滑洗凝脂。
侍儿扶起娇无力，
始是新承恩泽时。

The Everlasting Longing

Bai Juyi

The beauty-loving monarch longed year after year
To find a beautiful lady without a peer.
A maiden of the Yangs to womanhood just grown,
In inner chambers bred, to the world was unknown.
Endowed with natural beauty too hard to hide,
She was chosen one day to be the monarch's bride.
Turning her head, she smiled so sweet and full of grace
That she outshone in six palaces the fairest face.
She bathed in glassy water of Warm-fountain Pool,
Which laved and smoothed her creamy skin when spring was cool.
Without her maids' support, she was too tired to move,
And this was when she first received the monarch's love,

云鬓花颜金步摇，
芙蓉帐暖度春宵。
春宵苦短日高起，
从此君王不早朝。
承欢侍宴无闲暇，
春从春游夜专夜。
后宫佳丽三千人，
三千宠爱在一身。
金屋妆成娇侍夜，
玉楼宴罢醉和春。
姊妹弟兄皆列土，
可怜光彩生门户。
遂令天下父母心，
不重生男重生女。
骊宫高处入青云，
仙乐风飘处处闻。
缓歌慢舞凝丝竹，

Flower-like face and cloud-like hair, golden-headdressed.
In lotus-adorned curtain she spent the night blessed.
She slept till the sun rose high for the blessed night was short,
From then on the monarch held no longer morning court.
In revels as in feasts she shared her lord's delight,
His companion on trips and his mistress at night.
In inner palace dwelt three thousand ladies fair,
On her alone was lavished royal love and care.
Her beauty served the night when dressed up in Golden Bower,
She was drunk with wine and spring at banquet in Jade Tower.
Her sisters and brothers all received rank and fief,
And honors showered on her household, to the grief
Of fathers and mothers who would rather give birth
To a fair maiden than to any son on earth,
The lofty palace towered high into the cloud;
With divine music borne on the breeze the air was loud.
Seeing slow dance and hearing fluted or stringed song,

尽日君王看不足。
渔阳鼙鼓动地来，
惊破霓裳羽衣曲。
九重城阙烟尘生，
千乘万骑西南行。
翠华摇摇行复止，
西出都门百余里。
六军不发无奈何，
婉转蛾眉马前死。
花钿委地无人收，
翠翘金雀玉搔头。
君王掩面救不得，
回看血泪相和流。
黄埃散漫风萧索，
云栈萦纡登剑阁。
峨嵋山下少人行，
旌旗无光日色薄。

The emperor was never tired the whole day long.

But rebels beat their war drums, making the earth quake

And "*Song of Rainbow Skirt and Coat of Feathers*" break,

A cloud of dust was raised o'er city walls nine-fold;

Thousands of chariots and horsemen southwestward rolled.

Imperial flags moved slowly now and halted then,

And thirty miles from Western Gate they stopped again.

Six armies-what could be done-would not march with speed

Unless fair Lady Yang be killed before the steed.

None would pick up her hairpin fallen on the ground

Nor golden bird nor comb with which her head was crowned.

The monarch could not save her and hid his face in fear;

Turning his head, he saw her blood mix with his tear.

The yellow dust widespread, the wind blew desolate;

A serpentine plank path led to cloud-capped Sword Gate.

Below the Eyebrow Mountains wayfarers were few;

In fading sunlight royal standards lost their hue,

蜀江水碧蜀山青，
圣主朝朝暮暮情。
行宫见月伤心色，
夜雨闻铃肠断声。
天旋地转回龙驭，
到此踌躇不能去。
马嵬坡下泥土中，
不见玉颜空死处。
君臣相顾尽沾衣，
东望都门信马归。
归来池苑皆依旧，
太液芙蓉未央柳。
芙蓉如面柳如眉，
对此如何不泪垂。
春风桃李花开日，
秋雨梧桐叶落时。
西宫南内多秋草，

On Western water blue and Western mountains green
The monarch's heart was daily gnawed by sorrow keen.
The moon viewed from his tent shed a soul-searing light;
The bells heard in night rain made a heart-rending sound.
Suddenly turned the tide. Returning from his flight,
The monarch could not tear himself away from the ground
Where 'mid the clouds beneath the Slope he couldn't forget
The fair-faced Lady Yang who was unfairly slain.
He looked at his courtiers, with tears his robe was wet;
They rode east to the capital but with loose rein.
Come back, he found her pond and garden in old place,
With lotus in the lake and willows by the hall,
Willow leaves like her brows and lotus like her face,
At the sight of all these, how could his tears not fall?
Or when in vernal breeze were peach and plum full-blown
Or when in autumn rain parasol leaves were shed?
In Western as in Southern Court was grass o'ergrown;

落叶满阶红不扫。
梨园弟子白发新，
椒房阿监青娥老。
夕殿萤飞思悄然，
孤灯挑尽未成眠。
迟迟钟鼓初长夜，
耿耿星河欲曙天。
鸳鸯瓦冷霜华重，
翡翠衾寒谁与共。
悠悠生死别经年，
魂魄不曾来入梦。
临邛道士鸿都客，
能以精诚致魂魄。
为感君王辗转思，
遂教方士殷勤觅。
排空驭气奔如电，
升天入地求之遍。

With fallen leaves unswept the marble steps turned red,
Actors, although still young, began to have hair grey.
Eunuchs and waiting maids looked old in palace deep.
Fireflies flitting the hall, mutely he pined away;
The lonely lampwick bumed out, still he could not sleep.
Slowly beat drums and rang bells, night began to grow long;
Bright shone the Starry Stream, daybreak seemed to come late,
The lovebird tiles grew chilly with hoar frost so strong;
His kingfisher quilt was cold, not shared by a mate.
One long, long year the dead with the living was parted;
Her soul came not in dreams to see the broken-hearted.
A Taoist sorcerer came to the palace door,
Skilled to summon the spirits from the other shore.
Moved by the monarch's yearning for the departed fair,
He was ordered to seek for her everywhere.
Borne on the air, like flash of lightning flew;
In heaven and on earth he searched through and through.

上穷碧落下黄泉，
两处茫茫皆不见。
忽闻海上有仙山，
山在虚无缥缈间。
楼阁玲珑五云起，
其中绰约多仙子。
中有一人字太真，
雪肤花貌参差是。
金阙西厢叩玉扃，
转教小玉报双成。
闻道汉家天子使，
九华帐里梦魂惊。
揽衣推枕起徘徊，
珠箔银屏迤逦开。
云鬓半偏新睡觉，
花冠不整下堂来。
风吹仙袂飘飘举，

Up to the azure vault and down to deepest place,
Nor above nor below could he e'er find her trace.
He learned that on the sea were fairy mountains proud,
Which now appeared now disappeared amid the cloud
Of rainbow colors, where rose magnificent bowers
And dwelt so many fairies as graceful as flowers.
Among them was a queen whose name was Ever True;
Her snow-white skin and sweet face might afford a clue,
Knocking at western gate of palace hall, he bade
The fair porter to inform the queen's waiting maid,
When she heard that there came the monarch's embassy,
The queen was startled out of dreams in her canopy.
Pushing aside the pillow, she rose and got dressed,
Passing through silver screen and pearl shade to meet the guest.
Her cloud-like hair awry, not full awake at all,
Her flowery cap slanted, she came into the hall.
The wind blew up her fairy sleeves and made them float

犹似霓裳羽衣舞。
玉容寂寞泪阑干，
梨花一枝春带雨。
含情凝睇谢君王，
一别音容两渺茫。
昭阳殿里恩爱绝，
蓬莱宫中日月长。
回头下望人寰处，
不见长安见尘雾。
惟将旧物表深情，
钿合金钗寄将去。
钗留一股合一扇，
钗擘黄金合分钿。
但教心似金钿坚，
天上人间会相见。
临别殷勤重寄词，
词中有誓两心知。

As if she danced still "Rainbow Skirt and Feathered Coat."

Her jade-white face crisscrossed with tears in lonely world

Like a spray of pear blossoms in spring rain impearled.

She bade him thank her lord, lovesick and broken-hearted;

They knew nothing of each other after they parted,

Love and happiness long ended within palace walls;

Days and nights appeared long in the Fairyland halls.

Turning her head and fixing on the earth her gaze,

She found no capital 'mid clouds of dust and haze.

To show her love was deep, she took out keepsakes old

For him to carry back, hairpin and case of gold.

Keeping one side of the case and one wing of the pin;

She sent to her lord the other half of the twin.

"If our two hearts as firm as the gold should remain,

In heaven or on earth some time we'll meet again,"

At parting, she confided to the messenger

A secret vow known only to her lord and her.

七月七日长生殿，
夜半无人私语时。
在天愿作比翼鸟，
在地愿为连理枝。
天长地久有时尽，
此恨绵绵无绝期。

On seventh day of seventh moon when none was near,

At midnight in Long Life Hall he whispered in her ear:

"On high, we'd be two birds flying wing to wing;

On earth, two trees with branches twined from spring to spring."

The boundless sky and endless earth may pass away,

But this vow unfulfilled will be regretted for aye.

* *This long poem relates the life-and-death love story of Emperor Xuan Zong in the Tang Dynasty and his favorite Lady Yang Yuhuan.*

与浩初上人同看山寄京华亲故

柳宗元

海畔尖山似剑铓，
秋来处处割愁肠。
若为化得身千亿，
散上峰头望故乡。

Rocky Hills Viewed Together with Abbot Haochu

Liu Zongyuan

The seaside rocky hills look sharp like sword or dart;

They thrust out when autumn comes to cut and break my heart.

If I could be transformed into rocks, I would stand

Atop a thousand peaks to watch for my homeland.

* *The poet wishes to be transformed into a rock to watch for his homeland far away.*

雨后晓行独至愚溪北池

柳宗元

宿云散洲渚，
晓日明村坞。
高树临清池，
风惊夜来雨。
予心适无事，
偶此成宾主。

The Northern Pool Visited Alone after the Rain at Dawn

Liu Zongyuan

Over the islets disperse clouds of last night,

The rising sun makes poolside village bright.

A tall tree overlooks the water clear;

Raindrops fall, startled by the wind severe.

Unoccupied, my mind is just carefree;

By chance the tree plays host to welcome me.

* *The poet is as carefree as the tree by the poolside.*

溪居

柳宗元

久为簪组累，
幸此南夷谪。
闲依农圃邻，
偶似山林客。
晓耕翻露草，
夜榜响溪石。
来往不逢人，
长歌楚天碧。

Living by the Brookside

Liu Zongyuan

Tired of officialdom for long,

I'm glad to be banished southwest.

At leisure I hear farmer's song;

Haply I look like hillside guest.

At dawn I cut grass wet with dew;

My boat comes o'er pebbles at night.

To and fro there's no man in view;

I chant till southern sky turns bright.

* *The poet sings of his leisurely life after his banishment to the southwest.*

别舍弟宗一

柳宗元

零落残魂倍黯然，
双垂别泪越江边。
一身去国六千里，
万死投荒十二年。
桂岭瘴来云似墨，
洞庭春尽水如天。
欲知此后相思梦，
长在荆门郢树烟。

Farewell to My Younger Brother

Liu Zongyuan

Lonely, I feel more gloomy when I part with you;
Standing by riverside, we shed tears of adieu.
I am banished from home thousands of miles away;
Not dead for twelve long years, in the west land I stay.
Miasmic clouds darken the southern mountains high;
When spring ends on East lake, water blends with the sky.
From now on I would think of you and you of me;
I'd haunt in dreams our native land from tree to tree.

* *The poet reveals his homesickness while parting with his younger brother.*

城东早春

杨巨源

诗家清景在新春，
绿柳才黄半未匀。
若待上林花似锦，
出门俱是看花人。

Early Spring East of the Capital

Yang Juyuan

The early spring presents to poets a fresh scene:

The willow twigs half yellow and half tender green.

When the Royal Garden's covered with blooming flowers,

Then it would be the visitors' busiest hours.

* *This quatrain describes the beauty of spring scenery and the joy of visitors.*

马诗二十三首（其五）

李　贺

大漠沙如雪，
燕山月似钩。
何当金络脑，
快走踏清秋。

Horse Poems (V)

Li He

The desert sand looks white as snow;
The crescent moon hangs like a bow.
When would the steed in golden gear
Gallop all night through autumn clear?

* *The poet who cannot serve his country compares himself to a battle horse which cannot gallop at full speed.*

示　弟

李　贺

别弟三年后，
还家一日余。
醁醽今夕酒，
缃帙去时书。
病骨犹能在，
人间底事无。
何须问牛马，
抛掷任枭卢。

For My Younger Brother

Li He

I left three years ago;
Again I'm in my nooks.
Tonight green wine aglow,
I forget yellow books.
Ill, I survive at last.
What won't happen on earth?
Glad that the die is cast,
I'm free from care or mirth.

* *The poet writes this poem after his failure at civil service examinations.*

杨生青花紫石砚歌

李　贺

端州石工巧如神，
踏天磨刀割紫云。
佣刓抱水含满唇，
暗洒苌弘冷血痕。
纱帷昼暖墨花春，
轻沤漂沫松麝薰。
干腻薄重立脚匀，
数寸光秋无日昏。
圆毫促点声静新，
孔砚宽顽何足云！

The Violet Inkstand of Master Yang

Li He

The mason of Duanzhou has marvel-doing hands,
Whetting his knife to carve blue clouds, aloft he stands.
He grinds the stone in order to make an inkwell;
Violet flowers look dim like cold blood shed pell-mell.
Black flowers seem like spring at noon behind the screen;
The pine-soot ink steeped in water smells like musk keen.
Smooth, water-proof, flat and heavy, it stands steadfast;
Like autumn bright its color, rain or shine, will last.
Your brush will make no noise when on paper you write.
Could the inkstone of Confucius give such delight?

* *The poet glorifies the mason who carves violet clouds on the inkstand.*

将进酒

李　贺

琉璃钟，琥珀浓，
小槽酒滴真珠红。
烹龙炮凤玉脂泣，
罗帏绣幕围香风。
吹龙笛，
击鼍鼓；
皓齿歌，
细腰舞。
况是青春日将暮，
桃花乱落如红雨。
劝君终日酩酊醉，
酒不到刘伶坟上土！

Drinking Song

Li He

A glazed cup full of amber wine,
The strong drink drips like red pearls fine.
The dragon boiled and phoenix roasted would weep;
The fragrant breeze blows into broidered curtains deep.
The dragon flute is played;
Beaten the drums covered with alligator's skin.
The songstress sings with teeth as bright as jade,
And dancers dance with waist as slender as hairpin.
The prime of your life like the sun on the decline,
Peach blossoms fall pell-mell like rain of petals pink.
So I advise you to get drunk with wine.
When buried in the grave, what could you take to drink?

* *This imaginative song is full of sensual beauty. The reader may see amber wine and red pearls, hear the drink drip and the phoenix weep, smell the fragrant breeze and touch the dancer's slender waist and taste boiled dragon and roasted phoenix.*

官街鼓

李贺

晓声隆隆催转日，
暮声隆隆催月出。
汉城黄柳映新帘，
柏陵飞燕埋香骨。
磓碎千年日长白，
孝武秦王听不得。
从君翠发芦花色，
独共南山守中国。
几回天上葬神仙，
漏声相将无断缘。

Official Drums

Li He

At dawn official drumbeats hasten the sunrise;
At dusk the booming drums call the moon to the skies.
When yellow willows put forth new buds in the town,
In tomb is buried the favorite of the crown.
The drums have boomed a thousand years, still shines the sun,
But ancient emperors of Qin and Han have done.
Your hair once black may turn white as reed flowers stand,
The drums with southern hills will ever guard our land.
Even immortals were buried in the sky,
The drumbeats and the water-clock will never die.

* *The time-marking drumbeats, says the poet, will last longer than imperial dynasty and human life.*

致酒行

李　贺

零落栖迟一杯酒，
主人奉觞客长寿。
主父西游困不归，
家人折断门前柳。
吾闻马周昔作新丰客，
天荒地老无人识。
空将笺上两行书，
直犯龙颜请恩泽。
我有迷魂招不得，
雄鸡一声天下白。
少年心事当拏云，
谁念幽寒坐呜呃。

Drinking Song

Li He

Unsuccessful I stay but with a cup of wine;
The kind host wishes me to live to ninety-nine.
An ancient could not but stay in the west for long;
In vain his household waited with their willow song.
“A young talent often met with contemptuous eye,
Unknown on the old earth under the dreary sky.
You may write letters of two lines now and again,
And you may not court imperial favor in vain.”
I would not call back my soul lost in a sad plight,
But when the cock crows, all the world will see daylight.
“While young, you should aim high and soar into the cloud.
Who pities a lonely man sobbing in the crowd?”

金铜仙人辞汉歌并序

李　贺

魏明帝青龙元年八月，诏宫官牵车西取汉孝武捧露盘仙人，欲立置前殿。宫官既拆盘，仙人临载乃潸然泪下。唐诸王孙李长吉遂作《金铜仙人辞汉歌》。

茂陵刘郎秋风客，
夜闻马嘶晓无迹。
画栏桂树悬秋香，
三十六宫土花碧。
魏官牵车指千里，
东关酸风射眸子。
空将汉月出宫门，
忆君清泪如铅水。

The Bronze Statue Leaving Han Palace

Li He

The emperor was gone just like his autumn breeze;
At night his steed would neigh, at dawn no trace was seen.
By painted rails fragrance still wafts over laurel trees,
His thirty palaces overgrown with mosses green.
Wei eunuch drove a dray to go a long, long way;
In Eastern Pass the sour wind stung the bronze's eyes.
Only the moon of yore saw him leave palace door;
Thinking of his dear lord, he shed tears and heaved sighs.

衰兰送客咸阳道，
天若有情天亦老。
携盘独出月荒凉，
渭城已远波声小。

Withered orchid would say, "Farewell and go your way."

Heaven would have grown old if it could feel as man.

He went with moon-shaped plate beneath the moon desolate;

The waves unheard, far from the town the horses ran.

* *The Martial Emperor of the Han Dynasty, author of Ode to the Autumn Breeze. built a bronze statue with a moon-shaped plate, but the Bright Emperor of the Wei Dynasty ordered his eunuch to move it out of the palace, and the bronze was said to have shed tears. This poem shows the poet, like the bronze, is unwilling to leave the capital after his failure in the civil service examinations.*

秦王饮酒

李 贺

秦王骑虎游八极，
剑光照空天自碧。
羲和敲日玻璃声，
劫灰飞尽古今平。
龙头泻酒邀酒星，
金槽琵琶夜枨枨。
洞庭雨脚来吹笙，
酒酣喝月使倒行。
银云栉栉瑶殿明，
宫门掌事报一更。
花楼玉凤声娇狞，

The Drinking Song of the King of Qin

Li He

The King of Qin rode the tiger to eight Poles high;
His sword shone in the air and brightened the blue sky.
His driver struck the sun with a glass-breaking sound;
All were reduced to ashes on the battleground.
Stars were invited to drink wine poured from dragon's head;
The golden pipa played at night would grieve the dead.
The rain treading on Dongting Lake would blow the lute;
The King ordered the moon to go back to its root.
Silver cloud on cloud made the crystal palace bright;
The gate-keeper announced it was still early night.
The phoenix in the tower sang her bewitching song;

海绡红文香浅清，
黄鹅跌舞千年觥。
仙人烛树蜡烟轻，
清琴醉眼泪泓泓。

Clear fragrance of ladies' silken dress wafted long.

The dancers drank to his health of a thousand years.

From the candles on the fairy trees rose smoke light;

From the lutist's drunken eyes streamed down copious tears.

* *The poet imagines how the King of Qin drank like an immortal.*

老夫采玉歌

李　贺

采玉采玉须水碧，
琢作步摇徒好色。
老夫饥寒龙为愁，
蓝溪水气无清白。
夜雨冈头食蓁子，
杜鹃口血老夫泪。
蓝溪之水厌生人，
身死千年恨溪水。
斜山柏风雨如啸，
泉脚挂绳青袅袅。
村寒白屋念娇婴，
古台石磴悬肠草。

Song of an Old Jade-digger

Li He

He digs up jade, he digs up jade in water green
To make a headdress for a lady or a queen.
When he's hungry and cold, the dragon would be sad;
Nor clear nor pure, the water of Blue Creek turns bad.
He eats hazelnuts when it rains in mountains deep;
With tears like the blood shed by the cuckoo, he'd weep.
The Blue Creek dislikes a digger when he appears;
He too dislikes it though dead for a thousand years.
By the mountainside the wind soughs and the rain falls;
A rope hangs around his waist over waterfalls.
How can he not think of his children in his hut cold,
When he sees the forget-me-not on the cliff old?

* *The poet sympathizes with the poor old man who digs up jade from the Blue Creek.*

闻　雁

韦应物

故园眇何处，
归思方悠哉。
淮南秋雨夜，
高斋闻雁来。

On Hearing Homing Wild Geese

Wei Yingwu

My native land's far, far away,

My nostalgia grows day by day.

Alone on rainy autumn night

I hear homing wild geese in flight.

* *The poet longs for his home on hearing the home going wild geese.*

寒食寄京师诸弟

韦应物

雨中禁火空斋冷，
江上流莺独坐听。
把酒看花想诸弟，
杜陵寒食草青青。

For My Brothers in the Capital on Cold Food Day

Wei Yingwu

No fire is made in empty room on rainy days;
I hear alone the riverside orioles' lays.
Drinking, I gaze on flowers and miss my brothers dear;
On Cold Food Day homeland grass grows green and drear.

* *In ancient China the Cold Food Day fell three days ahead of the Mourning Day, that is, the fourth or fifth day in the third lunar month. No fire was made on Cold Food Day because an ancient sage burned himself in the mountains, so people would eat cold food in mourning for him.*

淮上喜会梁川故人

韦应物

江汉曾为客，
相逢每醉还。
浮云一别后，
流水十年间。
欢笑情如旧，
萧疏鬓已斑。
何因不归去，
淮上有秋山。

Meeting with Friends on River Huai

Wei Yingwu

We met on River Huai;
Not till drunk did we go.
We went as clouds float by;
In ten years waves still flow.
We laugh as in old days,
Though our hair has turned white.
Why don't I go away?
I love autumn hills bright.

* *Meet or part, the river will ever flow and the poet will ever love his homeland.*

淮上即事寄广陵亲故

韦应物

前舟已眇眇，
欲度谁相待。
秋山起暮钟，
楚雨连沧海。
风波离思满，
宿昔容鬓改。
独鸟下东南，
广陵何处在。

For Kinsfolk and Friends at Guangling

Wei Yingwu

Gone is the ferry boat.

Who'll carry me afloat?

At dusk uphill bell rings;

Over seaside rain sings.

Grief saddens the waves cold;

My face and hair look old.

Southeast flies a lone bird;

Your voices can't be heard.

* *The poet, lonely at the ferry on River Huai, thinks of kinsfolk and friends at Guangling.*

塞下曲六首（其二）

卢　纶

林暗草惊风，
将军夜引弓。
平明寻白羽，
没在石棱中。

Border Songs (II)

Lu Lun

In gloomy woods grass shivers at wind's howl;
The general takes it for a tiger's growl.
He shoots and looks for his arrow next morn
Only to find a rock pierced amid the thorn.

塞下曲六首（其三）

卢　纶

月黑雁飞高，
单于夜遁逃。
欲将轻骑逐，
大雪满弓刀。

Border Songs (III)

Lu Lun

Wild geese fly high in moonless night;
The Tartars through the dark take flight.
Our horsemen chase them, armed with bow
And sword covered with heavy snow.

* *The poet glorifies the cavaliers in pursuit of the foe on a snowy night.*

菊 花

元 稹

秋丛绕舍似陶家，
遍绕篱边日渐斜。
不是花中偏爱菊，
此花开尽更无花。

Chrysanthemums

Yuan Zhen

Around the cottage like Tao's autumn flowers grow;

Along the hedge I stroll until the sun slants low.

Not that I favor partially the chrysanthemum,

But it is the last flower after which none will bloom.

* *Tao refers to the poet Tao Yuanming, well-known for his love of chrysanthemums.*

重赠乐天

元　稹

休遣玲珑唱我诗，
我诗多是别君词。
明朝又向江头别，
月落潮平是去时。

Parting Again with Bai Juyi

Yuan Zhen

Don't let the songstress sing my songs anew!

Most of them are farewell poems for you.

Tomorrow again we'll part by riverside,

Alas! At moonset when outflows the tide.

* *The poet would not listen to farewell songs for they would bring to his mind farewells past and future.*

酬乐天频梦微之

元　稹

山水万重书断绝，
念君怜我梦相闻。
我今因病魂颠倒，
唯梦闲人不梦君。

Dream and No Dream

Yuan Zhen

Letters can't pass over thousands of mountains and streams.
How much I thank you for you have sent me your dreams.
I'm sorry that in illness I can't tell old friends from new;
I dream of indifferent people, but not you.

* *The poet who has not dreamed of his friend sends him as much friendship as his friend who has.*

离思五首（其四）

元　稹

曾经沧海难为水，
除却巫山不是云。
取次花丛懒回顾，
半缘修道半缘君。

Thinking of My Dear Departed (IV)

Yuan Zhen

No water's wide enough when you have crossed the sea;

No cloud is beautiful but that which crowns the peak.

I pass by flowers which fail to attract poor me;

Hail for your sake and half for Taoism I seek.

* *The poet no longer loves nature as before after the death of his dear wife but tries to seek consolation from Taoism.*

六年春遣怀八首（其二）

元　稹

检得旧书三四纸，
高低阔狭粗成行。
自言并食寻常事，
唯念山深驿路长。

Elegies on My Deceased Wife (II)

Yuan Zhen

I find three or four sheets of your letters fine;
The words of your handwriting often go out of line.
You cared not for your hunger every other day,
If I was fed in deep mountains on my long way.

* *The poet remembers his wife who would suffer hunger every other day to provide for him on his way in the mountains.*

遣悲怀三首（其二）

元稹

昔日戏言身后意，
今朝都到眼前来。
衣裳已施行看尽，
针线犹存未忍开。
尚想旧情怜婢仆，
也曾因梦送钱财。
诚知此恨人人有，
贫贱夫妻百事哀。

To My Deceased Wife (II)

Yuan Zhen

"What if one of us should die?" we said for fun one day;
But now it has come true and passed before my eyes.
I can't bear to see your clothes and give them away;
I seal your embroidery lest it should draw my sighs.
Remembering your kindness, I'm kind to our maids;
Dreaming of your bounty, I give bounties as before.
I know there is no mortal but returns to the shades,
But a poor couple like us have more to deplore.

遣悲怀三首（其三）

元　稹

闲坐悲君亦自悲，
百年都是几多时。
邓攸无子寻知命，
潘岳悼亡犹费辞。
同穴窅冥何所望，
他生缘会更难期。
唯将终夜长开眼，
报答平生未展眉。

To My Deceased Wife (III)

Yuan Zhen

Sitting idle, I grieve for myself as for you;
How many days are left for my declining years?
Another childless man fared better than I do;
Another widower lavished vain verse and tears.
Could I await a better fate than our same tomb?
Could you be born again and again be my wife?
With eyes unclosed all night long I'll lie in the gloom
To repay you for your unknit brows in your life.

* *The poet has written three poems for his deceased wife and two of them are selected here.*

送友人

薛　涛

水国蒹葭夜有霜，
月寒山色共苍苍。
谁言千里自今夕，
离梦杳如关塞长。

Farewell to a Friend

Xue Tao

Waterside reeds are covered with hoarfrost at night;

The green mountains are drowned in the cold blue moonlight.

Who says a thousand miles will separate us today?

My dream will follow you though you are far away.

* *The poetess shows her love by saying distance cannot separate friends in dreams.*

牡丹

薛 涛

去春零落暮春时，
泪湿红笺怨别离。
常恐便同巫峡散，
因何重有武陵期？
传情每向馨香得，
不语还应彼此知。
只欲栏边安枕席，
夜深闲共说相思。

To the Peony Flower

Xue Tao

Petal by petal you fell in late spring last year;
Since you are gone, my paper's wet with tear on tear.
I am afraid you'd vanish like cloud in a dream.
How can I wish to see you on Peach Blossom Stream?
Your fragrance sweet reveals you have a loving heart;
Your silence shows we know each other far apart.
By the side of your balustrade I'd only sleep;
To tell you how I long for you when night is deep.

* *This poems shows how deep the poetess loves the flower.*

新嫁娘词三首（其三）

王　建

三日入厨下，
洗手作羹汤。
未谙姑食性，
先遣小姑尝。

A Bride (III)

Wang Jian

Married three days, I go shy-faced
To cook a soup with hands still fair.
To meet my mother-in-law's taste,
I send to her daughter the first share.

* *This quatrain describes the psychology of a young bride.*

望夫石

王　建

望夫处，
江悠悠。
化为石，
不回头。
山头日日风复雨，
行人归来石应语。

The Woman Waiting for Her Husband

Wang Jian

Waiting for him alone
Where the river goes by,
She turns into a stone
Gazing with longing eye.
Atop the hill from day to day come wind and rain;
The stone should speak to see her husband come again.

* *The legend goes that a woman waiting for the return of her husband turned into a stone statue by the riverside. Thus the stone becomes a symbol of lovesickness.*

秋思赠远二首（其一）

王　涯

当年只自守空帷，
梦里关山觉别离。
不见乡书传雁足，
唯看新月吐蛾眉。

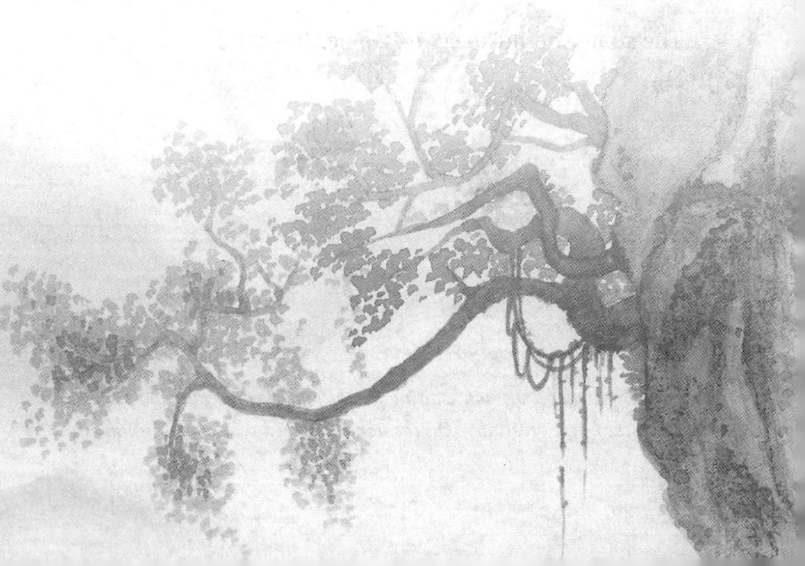

Autumn Thoughts for My Wife (I)

Wang Ya

In bygone years alone in empty room did I stay
To dream of the mountains of homeland far away.
Seeing no wild geese bringing me your letter now,
I only find the new moon like your arching brow.

秋思赠远二首（其二）

王　涯

厌攀杨柳临清阁，
闲采芙蕖傍碧潭。
走马台边人不见，
拂云堆畔战初酣。

Autumn Thoughts for My Wife (II)

Wang Ya

When tired of breaking willow branch before my bower,

I pluck at leisure by poolside the lotus flower.

I cannot find your face when I ride on my horse,

But hear the cloud echo war cries of combat force.

* *The poet in garrison on the frontier longs for his wife far away at home.*

幼女词

施肩吾

幼女才六岁，
未知巧与拙。
向夜在堂前，
学人拜新月。

Song of My Youngest Daughter

Shi Jianwu

My youngest daughter's six years old;
She cannot tell clumsy from clever.
At night on crossing the threshold,
She prays the moon to shine forever.

* *This quatrain describes the fond hope of the poet's six-year-old daughter.*

望夫词

施肩吾

手爇寒灯向影频，
回文机上暗生尘。
自家夫婿无消息，
却恨桥头卖卜人。

Longing for Her Husband

Shi Jianwu

Often looking back to her shadow by cold lamplight,

She only sees the dusty loom drowned in dark night.

Having never received news from her husband dear,

She blames the fortune-teller to say he'd appear.

* *The unreasonable blame shows the wife is eager to see her husband's return.*

悯农（其一）

李　绅

春种一粒粟，
秋收万颗子。
四海无闲田，
农夫犹饿死。

The Peasants (I)

Li Shen

Each seed when sown in spring,

Will make autumn yields high.

What will fertile fields bring?

Of hunger peasants die.

悯农（其二）

李　绅

锄禾日当午，
汗滴禾下土。
谁知盘中餐，
粒粒皆辛苦。

The Peasants (II)

Li Shen

At noon they weed with hoes;
Their sweat drips on the soil.
Each bowl of rice, who knows?
Is the fruit of hard toil.

* *The poet sympathizes with peasants who toil all the year around but die of hunger.*

长安秋望

杜　牧

楼倚霜树外，
镜天无一毫。
南山与秋色，
气势两相高。

Autumn in the Capital

Du Mu

The tower overlooks frosty trees;

Speckless is the mirror-like sky.

The South Mountain and autumn breeze

Vie to be more sublime and high.

赠别二首（其一）

杜　牧

娉娉袅袅十三余，
豆蔻梢头二月初。
春风十里扬州路，
卷上珠帘总不如。

At Parting (I)

Du Mu

Not yet fourteen, she's fair and slender
Like early budding flower tender.
Though Yangzhou Road's beyond compare,
Pearly screen uprolled, none's so fair.

赠别二首（其二）

杜　牧

多情却似总无情，
唯觉樽前笑不成。
蜡烛有心还惜别，
替人垂泪到天明。

At Parting (II)

Du Mu

Deep, deep our love, too deep to show;
Deep, deep we drink, silent we grow.
The candle grieves to see us part,
It melts in tears with burnt-out heart.

* *The poet describes his young love in Yangzhou as incomparable in the first quatrain and compares their heart to the burnt-out candle wick in the second.*

江南春

杜　牧

千里莺啼绿映红，
水村山郭酒旗风。
南朝四百八十寺，
多少楼台烟雨中。

Spring on the Southern Rivershore

Du Mu

Orioles sing for miles amid red blooms and green trees;
By hills and rills wine shop streamers wave in the breeze.
Four hundred eighty splendid temples still remain
Of Southern Dynasties in the mist and rain.

* *This quatrain shows the poet's admiration of the splendor of the Southern Rivershore.*

清　明

杜　牧

清明时节雨纷纷，
路上行人欲断魂。
借问酒家何处有，
牧童遥指杏花村。

The Mourning Day

Du Mu

A drizzling rain falls like tears on the Mourning Day;
The mourner's heart is going to break on his way.
Where can a wine shop be found to drown his sad hours?
A cowherd points to a cot amid apricot flowers.

* *On the Mourning Day early in the third moon, the mourner's tears mingle with the drizzling rain. This picture shows the commotion of man with nature.*

赤　壁

杜　牧

折戟沉沙铁未销，
自将磨洗认前朝。
东风不与周郎便，
铜雀春深锁二乔。

The Red Cliff

Du Mu

We dig out broken halberds buried in the sand
And wash and rub these relics of an ancient war.
Had the east wind refused General Zhou a helping hand,
His foe'd have locked his fair wife on Northern shore.

* *The Red Cliff was a scene of battle in 208 when General Zhou defeated the Northern enemy by setting their warships on fire with the help of the east wind.*

题乌江亭

杜　牧

胜败兵家事不期，
包羞忍耻是男儿。
江东子弟多才俊，
卷土重来未可知。

On the Black River Pavilion

Du Mu

A hero can't foretell victory or defeat.
Why should a loser not stand again on his feet?
There are so many talents on the Southern shore.
Who dare say, once defeated, he can't win the war?

* *The Herculean King of Chu, when defeated by the King of Han, killed himself on the Black River in 202 BC.*

题木兰庙

杜　牧

弯弓征战作男儿，
梦里曾经与画眉。
几度思归还把酒，
拂云堆上祝明妃。

Temple of the Heroine

Du Mu

She played the role of a man bending his bow,

But she dreamed of penciling her eyebrow.

How many times, homesick, wine cup in hand,

Would she bless the princess of her homeland?

* *The heroine refers to Hua Mulan who served in the army instead of her father, and the princess Wang Zhaojun who was married to the Chief of the Tartars in 33 BC.*

过华清宫绝句（其一）

杜　牧

长安回望绣成堆，
山顶千门次第开。
一骑红尘妃子笑，
无人知是荔枝来。

The Spring Palace (I)

Du Mu

Viewed from afar, the hill's paved with brocade in piles;
The palace doors on hilltops opened one by one.
A steed which raised red dust won the fair mistress' smiles.
How many steeds which brought her fruit died on the run!

过华清宫绝句（其二）

杜 牧

新丰绿树起黄埃，
数骑渔阳探使回。
霓裳一曲千峰上，
舞破中原始下来。

The Spring Palace (II)

Du Mu

Yellow dust raised by the steeds veiled trees like a screen;
The messenger deceived came to deceive the crown.
The Song of Rainbow Cloak over a thousand peaks green
Would not stop till the Central Plain was broken down.

* *The report said that General An Lushan would rise in revolt and the Bright Emperor sent messengers to An's headquarters, who, bribed by An, reported An's loyalty. The emperor deceived continued to enjoy the dance and music of Rainbow Cloak in the Spring Palace until the Central Plain was lost to An's revolting army in 755.*

叹　花

杜　牧

自是寻春去校迟，
不须惆怅怨芳时。
狂风落尽深红色，
绿叶成阴子满枝。

Sighing over Fallen Flowers

Du Mu

I regret to be late to seek for blooming spring;

The flowers not in full bloom in years past I've seen.

The strong wind blows down flowers which sway and swing,

The tree will be laden with red fruit and leaves green.

* *It was said that the poet met with a beautiful maiden and asked for her hand, but next year when he came she was married, so he compares the maiden to a tree with fruit.*

寄扬州韩绰判官

杜 牧

青山隐隐水迢迢，
秋尽江南草未凋。
二十四桥明月夜，
玉人何处教吹箫。

For Han Chuo, Judge of Yangzhou

Du Mu

The dreaming green hills stretch as far as the blue streams;
At autumn's end grass seems still green on southern shore.
Twenty-four fairies on the bridge steeped in moonbeams,
Are they still playing on the flute now as before?

* *This is a beautiful description of an autumn scene in Yangzhou.*

早雁

杜牧

金河秋半虏弦开，
云外惊飞四散哀。
仙掌月明孤影过，
长门灯暗数声来。
须知胡骑纷纷在，
岂逐春风一一回。
莫厌潇湘少人处，
水多菰米岸莓苔。

To the Early Wild Geese

Du Mu

The foe shoot arrows on frontier in autumn day;
The startled grieved wild geese disperse and fly away.
The statue sees their shadows pass beneath the moon bright;
The lonely palace hears their cries in candlelight.
You know the foe would run their horses therefore long.
Could you go back one and all when spring sings its song?
Don't say few live on Southern rivers up and down!
With water plants the Southern shores are overgrown.

* *The poet compares the refugees to the wild geese flying from north to south, for they also fled from the northern frontier occupied by the foe to the southern rivershore.*

宣州送裴坦判官往舒州，时牧欲赴官归京

杜　牧

日暖泥融雪半消，
行人芳草马声骄。
九华山路云遮寺，
清弋江村柳拂桥。
君意如鸿高的的，
我心悬旆正摇摇。
同来不得同归去，
故国逢春一寂寥。

Farewell to Pei Tan, Judge of Xuancheng, upon Going Back to the Capital

Du Mu

The snow in warming sun has half melted away;
You who will go on fragrant grass hear your horse neigh.
Over the mountain path clouds veil the temple drear;
The willow tips caress the bridge on River Clear.
Your ideal will fly up as high as the wild geese;
My mind still flutters like a streamer in the breeze.
Coming together, I cannot go back with you.
How lonely I'd feel at home when spring comes anew!

* *This poem depicts the scenery in the first half and the poet's mind in the second.*

题宣州开元寺水阁，阁下宛溪，夹溪居人

杜　牧

六朝文物草连空，
天澹云闲今古同。
鸟去鸟来山色里，
人歌人哭水声中。
深秋帘幕千家雨，
落日楼台一笛风。
惆怅无因见范蠡，
参差烟树五湖东。

Ruined Splendor

Du Mu

Rank grasses grow, six dynasties' splendors no more;
The sky is lightly blue and clouds free as of yore.
Birds come and go into the gloom of wooded hills,
And songs and wails alike merge in murmuring rills.
Like countless window curtains falls late autumn rain:
High towers steeped in sunset, wind and flute's refrain.
O how I miss the lakeside sage of bygone days!
I see but ancient trees loom rugged in the haze.

* *The poet describes the ruins to show his regret for the past splendor. The lakeside sage refers to General Fan who was said to have retired by the lakeside with the beautiful Lady of the West after his victory over the King of Wu in 473 BC.*

天　涯

李商隐

春日在天涯，
天涯日又斜。
莺啼如有泪，
为湿最高花。

The End of the Sky

Li Shangyin

Spring is far, far away

Where the sun slants its ray.

If orioles have tear,

Wet highest flowers here!

* *This quatrain may be said to be an elegy of spring, of the poet's life and of his era. The place is far away and the time late, even a happy bird would be saddened to shed tears on beautiful flowers.*

悼伤后赴东蜀辟至散关遇雪

李商隐

剑外从军远，
无家与寄衣。
散关三尺雪，
回梦旧鸳机。

Dreaming of My Deceased Wife at Her Loom

Li Shangyin

I join the army far away.
Who'd send me warm clothes for cold day?
The mountain pass is clad in snow;
My dream of her loom brings me woe.

* *The poet in the army dreams of his deceased wife on a cold day.*

乐游原

李商隐

向晚意不适，
驱车登古原。
夕阳无限好，
只是近黄昏。

On the Plain of Imperial Tombs

Li Shangyin

At dusk my heart is filled with gloom;

I drive my cab to ancient tomb.

The setting sun seems so sublime,

But it is near its dying time.

* *The Merry-making Plain was also called Plain of Imperial Tombs for emperors were buried there. The last two lines are proverbial as "He laughs best who laughs last."*

宿骆氏亭寄怀崔雍崔衮

李商隐

竹坞无尘水槛清，
相思迢递隔重城。
秋阴不散霜飞晚，
留得枯荷听雨声。

For the Cui Brothers at Luo's Pavilion

Li Shangyin

In the bamboo grove by the clean poolside I stay;
Separated from you by towns, I miss you far away.
The autumn gloom undispersed and late frost remain;
Only the withered lotus listen to the rain.

* *Passing one rainy night at Luo's Pavilion, the poet thought of the Cui brothers far away and wrote this quatrain which describes his gloomy mood rather than autumn gloom.*

霜　月

李商隐

初闻征雁已无蝉，
百尺楼高水接天。
青女素娥俱耐冷，
月中霜里斗婵娟。

Frost and Moon

Li Shangyin

No cicadas trill when I first hear wild geese cry;

The high tower overlooks water blending with the sky.

The Moon Goddess and her Maid of Frost are cold-proof;

They vie in beauty in moonlight over frosty roof.

* *Seeing the bright moon and frost, the poet imagines the Moon Goddess and her Maid of Frost are vying in beauty.*

柳

李商隐

曾逐东风拂舞筵，
乐游春苑断肠天。
如何肯到清秋日，
已带斜阳又带蝉。

To the Willow Tree

Li Shangyin

Having caressed the dancers in the vernal breeze,
You're ravished amid the merry-making trees.
How can you wail until clear autumn days are done
To shrill like poor cicadas in the setting sun?

* *The poet compares himself to the willow ravishing in spring and wailing in autumn.*

夜雨寄北

李商隐

君问归期未有期，
巴山夜雨涨秋池。
何当共剪西窗烛，
却话巴山夜雨时。

Written on a Rainy Night to My Wife in the North

Li Shangyin

You ask me when I can return, but I don't know;
It rains in western hills and autumn pools overflow.
When can we trim by window side the candlelight
And talk about the western hills in rainy night?

* *This poet answers his wife's question first by a picture and then by another question.*

为有

李商隐

为有云屏无限娇，
凤城寒尽怕春宵。
无端嫁得金龟婿，
辜负香衾事早朝。

A Nobleman's Wife

Li Shangyin

Behind the screen his wife is charming without peer,
But she's afraid the vernal night should be too short.
Why should she be wed to her noble lord so dear?
At early dawn he'd leave her pillow for the court.

* *This quatrain describes the sorrow of a nobleman's wife whose lord should rise early to go to court.*

嫦娥

李商隐

云母屏风烛影深，
长河渐落晓星沉。
嫦娥应悔偷灵药，
碧海青天夜夜心。

To the Moon Goddess

Li Shangyin

Upon the marble screen the candlelight is winking;
The Silver River slants and morning stars are sinking.
You'd regret to have stolen the miraculous potion;
Each night you brood over the lonely celestial ocean.

* *According to the myth, the archer who had shot down nine suns had miraculous potion, but his wife stole it, flew to the moon and became the lonely moon goddess.*

咏 史

李商隐

北湖南埭水漫漫，
一片降旗百尺竿。
三百年间同晓梦，
钟山何处有龙盘？

On History

Li Shangyin

Water shimmers in Northern Lake and by Southern Tower,
All kings surrendered with white flags to a new power.
Three hundred years have passed like a dream one and all;
No Coiling Dragon could keep kingdoms from downfall.

* *The Northern Lake, Southern Tower, Mount Coiling Dragon are all in the vicinity of the capital of the six dynasties, but neither mountains nor rivers could defend the kingdom against the invading power.*

谒山

李商隐

从来系日乏长绳，
水去云回恨不胜。
欲就麻姑买沧海，
一杯春露冷如冰。

Homage to the Mountain

Li Shangyin

Since olden days there is no rope to bind the sun.

How could we stop the cloud and water on the run?

I'd like to buy the vast sea from the goddess nice,

But a cup of spring dew soon turns as cold as ice.

韩冬郎即席为诗相送，一座尽惊。他日余方追吟“连宵侍坐徘徊久”之句，有老成之风，因成二绝寄酬，兼呈畏之员外（其一）

李商隐

十岁裁诗走马成，
冷灰残烛动离情。
桐花万里丹山路，
雏凤清于老凤声。

For Han Wo, Poet Prodigy (I)

Li Shangyin

You wrote a verse with highest speed at ten years old;
We would not part though candle ashes turned cold.
The flowery mountain path extends for miles long;
The young surpass the old in singing phoenix's song.

蝉

李商隐

本以高难饱，
徒劳恨费声。
五更疏欲断，
一树碧无情。
薄宦梗犹泛，
故园芜已平。
烦君最相警，
我亦举家清。

To the Cicada

Li Shangyin

High, you can't eat your fill;
In vain you wail and trill.
At dawn you hush your song;
The tree is green for long.
I drift as water flows;
And waste my garden grows.
Thank you for warning due,
I am as poor as you.

* *The poet compares himself to the poor, hungry cicada.*

落　花

李商隐

高阁客竟去，
小园花乱飞。
参差连曲陌，
迢递送斜晖。
肠断未忍扫，
眼穿仍欲稀。
芳心向春尽，
所得是沾衣。

Falling Flowers

Li Shangyin

The guest has left my tower high,

My garden flowers pell-mell fly.

Here and there over the winding way

They say goodbye to parting day.

I won't sweep them with broken heart,

But wish they would not fall apart.

Their love with spring won't disappear,

Each dewdrop turns into a tear.

* *The poet describes his gloomy mood on seeing the falling flowers.*

骄儿诗

李商隐

衮师我骄儿，
美秀乃无匹。
文葆未周晬，
固已知六七。
四岁知姓名，
眼不视梨栗。
交朋颇窥观，
谓是丹穴物。
前朝尚器貌，
流品方第一。
不然神仙姿，
不尔燕鹤骨。

Song of My Proud Son

Li Shangyin

I am proud of my son,

He is second to none.

Come down one year from Heaven,

He could tell six from seven.

Knowing his name at four,

No pears would he adore.

My friends would come and say

He is no common clay.

His appearance admired

Leaves nothing to be desired.

An immortal would fain

Say he's swallow or crane.

安得此相谓，
欲慰衰朽质。
青春妍和月，
朋戏浑甥侄。
绕堂复穿林，
沸若金鼎溢。
门有长者来，
造次请先出。
客前问所须，
含意不吐实。
归来学客面，
闹败秉爷笏。
或谑张飞胡，
或笑邓艾吃。
豪鹰毛崱屴，
猛马气佶傈。
截得青筼筜，

What my friends say, all told,

Would comfort a man old.

In vernal night or day

With his cousins he'd play.

They pass from hall to hall,

Boisterous one and all.

When guests come to see me,

He would come out with glee.

When asked what he need,

He'd veil the truth, indeed.

He mimics one guest's face

In haste and without grace,

Another bearded guest

Stammering without rest.

Like an eagle in flight

Or a strong steed in fight,

He rides a hobby horse

骑走恣唐突。
忽复学参军，
按声唤苍鹘。
又复纱灯旁，
稽首礼夜佛。
仰鞭罥蛛网，
俯首饮花蜜。
欲争蛱蝶轻，
未谢柳絮疾。
阶前逢阿姊，
六甲颇输失。
凝走弄香奁，
拔脱金屈戌。
抱持多反侧，
威怒不可律。
曲躬牵窗网，
衉唾拭琴漆。

Running with all its force.

He jeers at officers

Blaming their messengers.

By lamplight he makes vows

And to Buddha he bows.

He sweeps webs with his whip,

And honey he would sip.

As light as butterflies,

With willow down he vies.

Meeting his sister dear,

He plays games without fear.

He takes her toilet box

And breaks the golden locks.

Lying on ground, he'd stay;

Threatened, he'd not obey.

He draws the window screen,

Spits and wipes the lute clean.

有时看临书，
挺立不动膝。
古锦请裁衣，
玉轴亦欲乞。
请爷书春胜，
春胜宜春日。
芭蕉斜卷笺，
辛夷低过笔。
爷昔好读书，
恳苦自著述。
憔悴欲四十，
无肉畏蚤虱。
儿慎勿学爷，
读书求甲乙。
穰苴司马法，
张良黄石术。
便为帝王师，

Sometimes watching me write,

He stands unmoved upright.

Of brocade he makes cover;

Of books he seems a lover.

Asking me to write "spring",

Of spring day he would sing.

Banana's paper white,

Its bud a brush to write.

Then I was fond of books,

Studying long in my nooks.

At forty lean and wise,

I fear nor bug nor lice.

Do not learn to win fame,

Like me without a name.

Try to learn from the sages

Of the different ages!

You'd be master of kings,

不假更纤悉。
况今西与北，
羌戎正狂悖。
诛赦两未成，
将养如痼疾。
儿当速成大，
探雏入虎穴。
当为万户侯，
勿守一经帙。

Carefree from trifling things.

The foe in the northwest

Are producing unrest.

Nor war nor peace can cure;

They're hard disease, for sure.

Grow up, be man of men.

Kill the foe in the den!

Son, be a hero brave

And not a scholar grave.

* *The poet describes in detail the son he is proud of and he lays his hope on.*

无　题

李商隐

相见时难别亦难，
东风无力百花残。
春蚕到死丝方尽，
蜡炬成灰泪始干。
晓镜但愁云鬓改，
夜吟应觉月光寒。
蓬山此去无多路，
青鸟殷勤为探看。

To One Unnamed

Li Shangyin

It's difficult for us to meet and hard to part;
The east wind is too weak to revive flowers dead.
Spring silkworm till its death spins silk from love-sick heart;
A candle but when burned out has no tears to shed.
At dawn I'm grieved to think your mirrored hair turns grey;
At night you would feel cold while I croon by moonlight.
To the three fairy hills it is not a long way.
Would the blue birds oft fly to see you on the height?

* *The poet writes this poem for his unnamed lover compared to a fairy living in the three mountains on the sea where only the mythical blue birds could bring messages.*

无题四首（其一）

李商隐

来是空言去绝踪，
月斜楼上五更钟。
梦为远别啼难唤，
书被催成墨未浓。
蜡照半笼金翡翠，
麝薰微度绣芙蓉。
刘郎已恨蓬山远，
更隔蓬山一万重。

Untitled Poems (I)

Li Shangyin

You said you'd come but you have gone and left no trace;
I hear in the moonlit tower the fifth watch bell.
In dream my cry could not call you back from distant place;
In haste with ink unthickened I cannot write well.
The candlelight illuminates half our broidered bed;
The smell of musk still faintly sweetens lotus screen.
Beyond my reach the far-off fairy mountains spread;
But you're still farther off than fairy mountains green.

* *The poet writes for one unnamed lover who passed sweet nights together with him.*

无题二首（其一）

李商隐

昨夜星辰昨夜风，
画楼西畔桂堂东。
身无彩凤双飞翼，
心有灵犀一点通。
隔座送钩春酒暖，
分曹射覆蜡灯红。
嗟余听鼓应官去，
走马兰台类转蓬。

Untitled Poems (I)

Li Shangyin

As last night twinkle stars, as last night blows the breeze,

West of the painted bower, east of Cassia Hall.

Having no wings I can't fly to you as I please;

Our hearts at one, your ears can hear my inner call.

Maybe you're playing hook in palm and drinking wine

Or guessing what the cup hides under candle red,

Alas! I hear the drum call me to duties mine;

Like rootless weed to Orchid Hall I ride ahead.

* *The poet who works in Orchid Hall and lives in Cassia Hall recalls the night spent together with his unnamed lover and imagines what she is doing on his lonely night.*

正月崇让宅

李商隐

密锁重关掩绿苔，
廊深阁迥此徘徊。
先知风起月含晕，
尚自露寒花未开。
蝙拂帘旌终展转，
鼠翻窗网小惊猜。
背灯独共余香语，
不觉犹歌《起夜来》。

Our Old Abode—Elegy on My Deceased Wife

Li Shangyin

Doors locked, curtains drawn down, on the mossy ground,
In winding corridor alone I stroll around.
By lunar halo the rising wind is foretold.
How can the flowers bloom when drenched in dew cold?
I toss in bed when curtain's hit by a bat;
I am surprised to hear in the net squeak a rat.
Alone I talk with your shadow by the lamplight.
How can I help singing with you "Rising at Night"?

* *The poet describes the dreary old abode after his wife's death.*

马嵬二首（其二）

李商隐

海外徒闻更九州，
他生未卜此生休。
空闻虎旅鸣宵柝，
无复鸡人报晓筹。
此日六军同驻马，
当时七夕笑牵牛。
如何四纪为天子，
不及卢家有莫愁？

On Lady Yang's Death (II)

Li Shangyin

Tis said there is a fairyland over the sea.
When this life is no more, can there another be?
In vain the watchman beat at night the warning gong;
No cock would wake her from dream with morning song.
The six armies demanded her death left and right.
Could she still laugh at severed lover-stars at night?
Though the emperor reigned as long as forty years,
She's not so happy as a griefless maid appears.

* *Lady Yang was the favorite mistress of the Bright Emperor of the Tang Dynasty. When the six armies in revolt demanded her death, the emperor could not protect her.*

安定城楼

李商隐

迢递高城百尺楼，
绿杨枝外尽汀洲。
贾生年少虚垂涕，
王粲春来更远游。
永忆江湖归白发，
欲回天地入扁舟。
不知腐鼠成滋味，
猜意鹓雏竟未休。

On the Tower of the City Wall

Li Shangyin

From hundred-foot-high city wall I look afar;
Beyond green willow trees the sandy islets are.
I remember a scholar while young shed vain tears,
And a famed scholar roamed in the spring of his years.
I can't forget white-haired General on the lake floating,
After changing the face of the world he went boating.
An owl might feed on dead rats with good appetite,
But a phoenix would perch on trees of lofty height.

锦　瑟

李商隐

锦瑟无端五十弦，
一弦一柱思华年。
庄生晓梦迷蝴蝶，
望帝春心托杜鹃。
沧海月明珠有泪，
蓝田日暖玉生烟。
此情可待成追忆，
只是当时已惘然。

The Sad Zither

Li Shangyin

Why should the sad zither have fifty strings?
Each string, each strain evokes but vanished springs:
Dim morning dream to be a butterfly;
Amorous heart poured out in cuckoo's cry.
In moonlit pearls see tears in mermaid's eyes;
From sunburnt jade in Blue Field let smoke rise.
Such feeling cannot be recalled again;
It seemed lost even when it was felt then.

* *The zither evokes vanished springs dim and free as the dream of a butterfly, amorous as the heart of a cuckoo, tearful as moonlit pearls and vaporous as the smoke rising from sunburnt jade in the Blue Field.*

鸣筝

李端

鸣筝金粟柱，
素手玉房前。
欲得周郎顾，
时时误拂弦。

The Golden Zither

Li Duan

How clear the golden zither rings

When her fair fingers touch its strings!

To draw attention from her lord,

Now and then she strikes a discord.

* *This quatrain speaks of music and the musician.*

闺情

李端

月落星稀天欲明，
孤灯未灭梦难成。
披衣更向门前望，
不忿朝来鹊喜声。

A Wife Longing for Her Husband

Li Duan

The stars are sparse when sinks the moon before daybreak;
The lonely lamplight not yet quenched, she lies awake.
Not dressed up, opening the door with longing eyes,
She complains of the false news announced by magpies.

* *It was believed in China that magpies would announce happy news, i.e., the return of the husband.*

观祈雨

李　约

桑条无叶土生烟，
箫管迎龙水庙前。
朱门几处看歌舞，
犹恐春阴咽管弦。

Praying for Rain

Li Yue

No leaves sprout from mulberry trees on drought-scorched earth;
Flutes and pipes are played to evoke the Rain God's mirth.
But the rich see dances and hear songstresses sing;
They only fear rain clouds would damage their lute string.

* *This quatrain makes a contrast between the poor praying for rain and the rich afraid the rain would spoil their pleasure.*

喜外弟卢纶见宿

司空曙

静夜四无邻，
荒居旧业贫。
雨中黄叶树，
灯下白头人。
以我独沉久，
愧君相见频。
平生自有分，
况是蔡家亲。

My Cousin Lu Lun's Visit

Sikong Shu

I feel lonely on quiet night,
A poor scholar in a sad plight.
A yellow-leafed tree in the rain,
By lamplight but white hairs remain.
Alone I have sunk low for long,
Still you would come to hear my song.
It's fate for us to meet or part,
But we are cousins dear at heart.

* *The poor poet is happy at his cousin's visit.*

夏夜宿表兄话旧

窦叔向

夜合花开香满庭，
夜深微雨醉初醒。
远书珍重何曾达，
旧事凄凉不可听。
去日儿童皆长大，
昔年亲友半凋零。
明朝又是孤舟别，
愁见河桥酒幔青。

Talking with My Cousin One Summer Night

Dou Shuxiang

The courtyard's fragrant with flowers blowing at night;

When night is deep, we wake from wine in drizzling rain.

We've not received from far away letters we write;

It's hard to talk about the bygone days with pain.

The children of the past have all grown tall and high;

Half of our friends and kinsmen are gone and departed.

Tomorrow when my lonely boat bids you goodbye,

Can we, seeing the streamers, not be broken-hearted?

* *The poet, appreciated by the premier, was transferred after the premier's dismissal.*

旅次朔方

刘 皂

客舍并州已十霜，
归心日夜忆咸阳。
无端又渡桑乾水，
却望并州似故乡。

Farther North

Liu Zao

Ten long, long winters in northern town I did stay;

My heart cried out for my southern home night and day.

Now as I cross the river, farther north I roam;

My heart cries out for northern town as for my home.

* *This quatrain describes well a roamer's psychology.*

江南曲

于　鹄

偶向江边采白蘋，
还随女伴赛江神。
众中不敢分明语，
暗掷金钱卜远人。

Song of the Southern Shore

Yu Hu

By riverside I pick white duckweed in company;
And watch the divine procession carelessly.
As I dare not show that for my husband I yearn,
I cast a coin aside to know when he'll return.

* *This poem describes a woman eager to see the return of her husband.*

题都城南庄

崔　护

去年今日此门中，
人面桃花相映红。
人面不知何处去，
桃花依旧笑春风。

Written in a Village South of the Capital

Cui Hu

In this house on this day last year a pink face vied
In beauty with the pink peach blossom side by side.
I do not know today where the pink face has gone;
In vernal breeze still smile pink peach blossoms full blown.

* *This quatrain is written in memory of a beauty the poet met with in the preceding year.*

忆扬州

徐　凝

萧娘脸薄难胜泪，
桃叶眉尖易觉愁。
天下三分明月夜，
二分无赖是扬州。

To One in Yangzhou

Xu Ning

Your bashful face could hardly bear the weight of tears;

Your long, long brows would easily feel sorrow nears.

Of all the moonlit nights on earth when people part,

Two-thirds shed sad light on Yangzhou with broken heart.

* *The poet regrets his parting from his lover in Yangzhou so much that he feels the moon heart-broken to see them part, and thus the place is beautified by their parting.*

塞下曲

许　浑

夜战桑乾北，
秦兵半不归。
朝来有乡信，
犹自寄寒衣。

Frontier Song

Xu Hun

In snow our men did fight,

Half of them died at night.

But letters came next day:

Winter clothes on the way.

途经秦始皇墓

许　浑

龙盘虎踞树层层，
势入浮云亦是崩。
一种青山秋草里，
路人唯拜汉文陵。

Passing by the Tomb of the First Emperor of the Qin Dynasty

Xu Hun

The dragon coils and tiger crouches amid the trees;

The sky-scraping imperial tomb can't but fall down.

The hill's still green with grass when blows the autumn breeze,

But the passers-by worship only the new crown.

金陵怀古

许　浑

玉树歌残王气终，
景阳兵合戍楼空。
松楸远近千官冢，
禾黍高低六代宫。
石燕拂云晴亦雨，
江豚吹浪夜还风。
英雄一去豪华尽，
唯有青山似洛中。

Memories of Jinling

Xu Hun

The kingdom collapsed after the Song of Jade Tree;

The garrison deserted when came the enemy.

Planted with pines, a thousand tombs spread far and nigh;

Buried amid the weed, palaces stand low and high.

The swallow of stone scrapes the white cloud, rain or shine;

The night breeze blows with waves raised by the river swine.

The splendor fades when heroes are gone one and all;

Only green hills look like the ancient capital.

* *Jinling was the capital of the six dynasties. The last king of Chen, author of the Song of Jade Tree, surrendered and the kingdom collapsed in 589. The swallow of stone was a statue in the palace and the river swine was said to be capable of raising waves.*

汴河亭

许　浑

广陵花盛帝东游，
先劈昆仑一派流。
百二禁兵辞象阙，
三千宫女下龙舟。
凝云鼓震星辰动，
拂浪旗开日月浮。
四海义师归有道，
迷楼还似景阳楼。

Royal Pavilion on the Great Canal

Xu Hun

The emperor went east to see the flowering town;
Mount Kunlun was cleft to let its water flow down.
Royal escorts leaving the palace went afloat;
Three thousand maids of honor mounted the dragon boat.
Drums were beaten to make clouds tremble and stars shiver;
Flags caressed waves, sun and moon floated on the river.
But by revolting armies the empire overthrown,
The emperor in the pavilion lost his crown.

* *This is a satire against the last emperor of the Sui Dynasty who lost his crown in 618.*

黄陵庙

李群玉

小姑洲北浦云边，
二女容华自俨然。
野庙向江春寂寂，
古碑无字草芊芊。
风回日暮吹芳芷，
月落山深哭杜鹃。
犹似含颦望巡狩，
九疑如黛隔湘川。

The Temple of Emperor Shun's Wives

Li Qunyu

North of the Maiden's Islet, by the riverside,
The two princesses shed tears in attire dignified.
The temple faces the river in lonely spring.
What could the wordless monument amid grass sing?
At sunset blows the breeze among the clovers white;
The cuckoos cry in hills from moon-down till deep night.
The princesses seem to gaze on Nine Peaks in dream,
Where was buried their emperor beyond the stream.

* *Emperor Shun was buried at the foot of the Nine Mysterious Peaks and his two wives came to weep over him by the riverside, where a temple was built in his memory.*

咏 史

戎 昱

汉家青史上，
计拙是和亲。
社稷依明主，
安危托妇人。
岂能将玉貌，
便拟静胡尘。
地下千年骨，
谁为辅佐臣。

On Appeasement by Marriage

Rong Yu

The kings in history sank so low
As to appease by marriage the foe.
To rule is a sovereign's duty.
Can safety depend on a beauty?
Could a face beautiful as jade
Repel the Tartars who invade?
Why were no loyal generals found
Among bones buried underground?

* *This is a satire against the kings who sought appeasement by marriage.*

金缕衣

无名氏

劝君莫惜金缕衣，
劝君须惜少年时。
有花堪折直须折，
莫待无花空折枝。

The Golden Dress

Anonymous

Love not your golden dress, I pray,
More than your youthful golden hours.
Gather sweet blossoms while you may,
And not the twig devoid of flowers!

剑　客

贾　岛

十年磨一剑，
霜刃未曾试。
今日把示君，
谁有不平事？

A Swordsman

Jia Dao

I've sharpened my sword for ten years;

I do not know if it will pierce.

I show its blade to you today.

O who has any grievance? Say!

雪晴晚望

贾　岛

倚杖望晴雪，
溪云几万重。
樵人归白屋，
寒日下危峰。
野火烧冈草，
断烟生石松。
却回山寺路，
闻打暮天钟。

Evening View of a Snow Scene

Jia Dao

Cane in hand, I gaze on fine snow;
Cloud on cloud spreads over the creek.
To snow-covered cots woodmen go;
The sun sets on the frowning peak.
In the wildfire bums the grass dried;
Mid rocks and pines smoke and mist rise.
Back to the temple by the hillside,
I hear bells ring in evening skies.

* *This poem is written after the poet's failure in the civil service examinations.*

秋寄从兄贾岛

无　可

暝虫喧暮色，
默思坐西林。
听雨寒更彻，
开门落叶深。
昔因京邑病，
并起洞庭心。
亦是吾兄事，
迟回共至今。

Written in Autumn for My Cousin Jia Dao

Wu Ke

The crickets' chirp breaks twilight late;

In the West Wood I meditate.

I hear a shower cold which grieves,

But outdoors I see fallen leaves.

The capital's weal and woe wake

Our dream to float on Dongting Lake.

Sink or swim, you will go your way;

You won't come back but go astray.

* *The poet, a monk, advises his cousin who was once a monk too, to float on the lake after his failure in the civil service examinations and not to go astray once more.*

商山早行

温庭筠

晨起动征铎，
客行悲故乡。
鸡声茅店月，
人迹板桥霜。
槲叶落山路，
枳花明驿墙。
因思杜陵梦，
凫雁满回塘。

Early Departure on Mount Shang

Wen Tingyun

At dawn I rise, with ringing bells my cab goes,
But grieved in thoughts of my home, I feel lost.
As the moon sets over thatched inn, the cock crows;
Footprints are left on wood bridge paved with frost.
The mountain path is covered with oak leaves,
The post-house bright with blooming orange trees.
The dream of my homeland last night still grieves,
A pool of mallards playing with wild geese.

* *This poem reveals the poet's homesickness by describing the scenery.*

苏武庙

温庭筠

苏武魂销汉使前，
古祠高树两茫然。
云边雁断胡天月，
陇上羊归塞草烟。
回日楼台非甲帐，
去时冠剑是丁年。
茂陵不见封侯印，
空向秋波哭逝川。

Temple of Su Wu

Wen Tingyun

How could Su Wu, before the envoi, not shed tears?
The ancient temple and tree bespeak bygone years.
Wild geese flew into clouds in moonlit Northern sky;
The sheep returned to west of frontier when grass grew high.
The palace looked unlike that of olden day;
Su was no longer strong as when he went away.
Ennobled when the emperor was in the grave,
He wept in vain over him gone with the autumn wave.

* *Su Wu (140BC—60BC) was an envoi retained by the Tartars for eighteen years. He was ennobled on his return when the emperor who sent him to the Tartars was dead. A temple was built in honor of Su's loyalty.*

馆娃宫怀古五绝（其一）

皮日休

绮阁飘香下太湖，
乱兵侵晓上姑苏。
越王大有堪羞处，
只把西施赚得吴。

The Palace of the Beauty (I)

Pi Rixiu

Her dress shed fragrance on the lake;

The Southern soldiers took the capital at daybreak.

It would be a shame for the Southern king to win

The Eastern Kingdom by a lady fair and thin.

* *The King of the Southern Yue, defeated by the Eastern King of Wu, offered a beautiful lady of the west, the Beauty to him, who loved her so much as to lose his kingdom in 473 BC.*

汴河怀古（其二）

皮日休

尽道隋亡为此河，
至今千里赖通波。
若无水殿龙舟事，
共禹论功不较多。

The Great Canal (II)

Pi Rixiu

The Great Canal was blamed for the Sui Empire's fall,

But on its waves the goods and food are brought to all.

Could the flood-fighting emperor do anything more

Than the Sui dragon-boats of three stories or four?

* *Emperor Yang of the Sui Dynasty (581—618) built the Great Canal and dragon-boats for pleasure-making, but it would facilitate the transportation and communication between North and South, and the poet praises him as high as the flood-fighting Emperor Yu of the Xia Dyansty (ca.2000 BC)*

白莲

陆龟蒙

素蘤多蒙别艳欺，
此花端合在瑶池。
无情有恨何人觉，
月晓风清欲堕时。

White Lotus

Lu Guimeng

White lotus blooms are often outweighed by red flowers;

They'd rather be transplanted before lunar bowers.

Heartless they seem, but they have deep grief no one knows.

See them fall in moonlight when the morning wind blows.

* *The poet describes the pure spirit of the white lotus blooms.*

别 离

陆龟蒙

丈夫非无泪，
不洒离别间。
杖剑对尊酒，
耻为游子颜。
蝮蛇一螫手，
壮士即解腕。
所志在功名，
离别何足叹。

Parting

Lu Guimeng

A hero may shed tears,

Not when parting with peers.

Sword in hand, he drinks wine,

Unlike roamers who pine.

When bitten by the snake,

He would have his wrist break.

With his career at heart,

He won't regret to part.

* *This poem talks about heroic parting.*

送日本国僧敬龙归

韦 庄

扶桑已在渺茫中，
家在扶桑东更东。
此去与师谁共到，
一船明月一帆风。

Farewell to a Japanese Monk

Wei Zhuang

The land of mulberry is in the boundless sea;

Your home's farther east to the land of mulberry.

Who would arrive with you at the land of your dreams?

A sail unfurled in wind, a boat steeped in moonbeams.

* *Japan was called the land of mulberry.*

小　松

杜荀鹤

自小刺头深草里，
而今渐觉出蓬蒿。
时人不识凌云木，
直待凌云始道高。

The Young Pine

Du Xunhe

While young, the pine tree thrusts its head amid tall grass;

Now by and by we find it outgrow weed in mass.

People don't realize it will grow to scrape the sky;

Seeing it tower in cloud, then they know it's high.

* *The poet satirizes people's lack of foresight.*

送友游吴越

杜荀鹤

去越从吴过，
吴疆与越连。
有园多种桔，
无水不生莲。
夜市桥边火，
春风寺外船。
此中偏重客，
君去必经年。

Seeing a Friend Off to the South

Du Xunhe

You go from north to south,

From land to river mouth.

Oranges in gardens loom;

Lotus on water bloom.

The night fair's bright as day;

Outside temples boats stay.

Welcome from far and near

Would make you stay a year.

* *This is a beautiful description of the Southern Rivershore.*

鹦鹉

罗隐

莫恨雕笼翠羽残，
江南地暖陇西寒。
劝君不用分明语，
语得分明出转难。

To the Parrot

Luo Yin

Do not complain of golden cage and wings cut short;
The southern land is far warmer than the northwest.
Don't clearly speak if you listen to my exhort;
You will offend if clearly your complaint's expressed.

* *This is a satire against clear complaint for fear of offence.*

金钱花

罗　隐

占得佳名绕树芳，
依依相伴向秋光。
若教此物堪收贮，
应被豪门尽劚将。

To the Coinlike Golden Flower

Luo Yin

You grow around a tree with a name bright,
You cling together steeped in autumn light.
If your flowers could be stored up like gold,
The rich would pluck you down since days of old.

* *This quatrain is a satire against man's greed for gold.*

柳

罗　隐

灞岸晴来送别频，
相偎相依不胜春。
自家飞絮犹无定，
争解垂丝绊路人？

To the Willow

Luo Yin

By riverside you see lovers part on fine day;
They cling together but they cannot make spring stay.
Your catkins waft in the breeze when your branches sway,
Could you retain those who are going far away?

* *The poet regrets neither he nor the willow could retain parting lovers.*

蜂

罗隐

不论平地与山尖，
无限风光尽被占。
采得百花成蜜后，
为谁辛苦为谁甜？

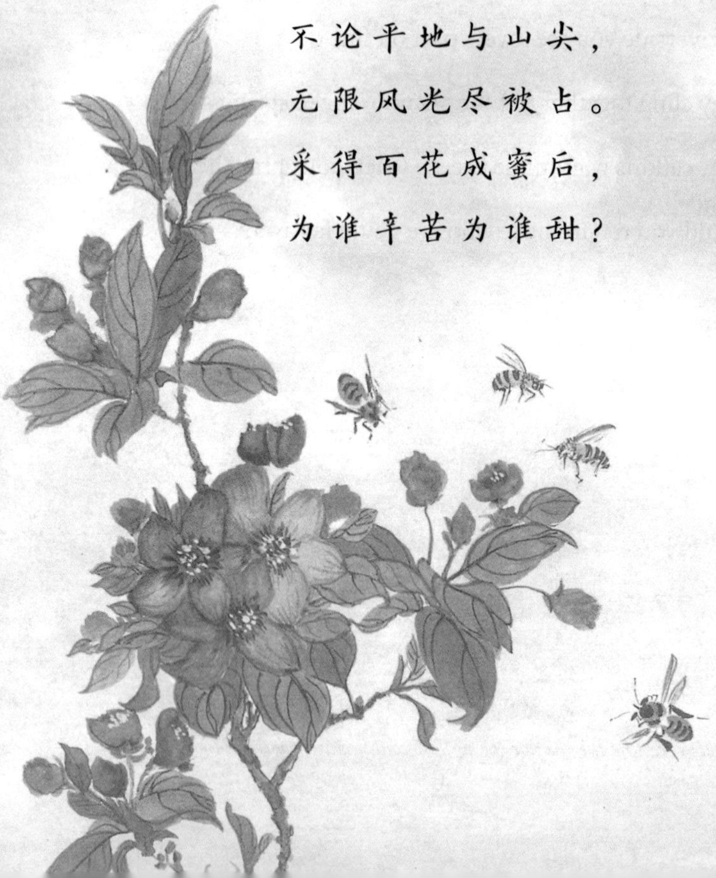

To the Bee

Luo Yin

On the plain or atop the hill,

Of beauty you enjoy your fill.

You gather honey from flowers sweet.

For whom are you busy and fleet?

* *The poet complains of the labor lost of the bee.*

黄　河

罗　隐

莫把阿胶向此倾，
此中天意固难明。
解通银汉应须曲，
才出昆仑便不清。
高祖誓功衣带小，
仙人占斗客槎轻。
三千年后知谁在，
何必劳君报太平？

The Yellow River

Luo Yin

Don’t try to make the muddy Yellow River clean!
Could Heaven mirrored in the waves be clearly seen?
How could a winding stream go up the Milky Way?
Just out of Mount Kunlun, it is muddy like clay.
In vain the emperor swore to narrow it down;
Could a raft reach the Polar Star wearing a crown?
Who knows if it will clear up after three thousand years?
Why should you worry if clear or not it appears?

* *The poet satirizes the imperial government as the muddy Yellow River which could not be made clean, for it was muddy from its source.*

菊

郑　谷

王孙莫把比蓬蒿，
九日枝枝近鬓毛。
露湿秋香满池岸，
由来不羡瓦松高。

To the Chrysanthemum

Zheng Gu

Do not compare your leaves with tumbleweed in hue!
On Mountain-climbing Day our head's adorned with you.
When poolside shores are sweet with your blooms wet with dew,
None envy pine-like plants high on the eaves in view.

* *The poet says that the chrysanthemum is incomparable.*

鹧 鸪

郑 谷

暖戏烟芜锦翼齐，
品流应得近山鸡。
雨昏青草湖边过，
花落黄陵庙里啼。
游子乍闻征袖湿，
佳人才唱翠眉低。
相呼相应湘江阔，
苦竹丛深日向西。

To the Partridges

Zheng Gu

Over warm misty grassland wing to wing you fly,
As fair and good as pheasants in the mountain high.
When Grass-green Lake is darkened in rain, you pass by;
When flowers fall on the Imperial Tomb, you cry.
A roamer would wet his sleeves with tears on hearing your song;
His wife'd sing after you with lowered eyebrows long.
You echo each other on Southern River wide;
The sun sets on the bamboo grove by the Tombside.

* *The partridge seems to cry in Chinese: "Don't go, brother!" The Imperial Tomb refers to the tomb of Emperor Shun who died by the side of the Grass-green Lake and whose wife came to shed tears on the bamboos by the tombside till they were specked.*

海　棠

郑　谷

春风用意匀颜色，
销得携觞与赋诗。
秾丽最宜新著雨，
娇娆全在欲开时。
莫愁粉黛临窗懒，
梁广丹青点笔迟。
朝醉暮吟看不足，
羡他蝴蝶宿深枝。

To the Crabapple Flower

Zheng Gu

The vernal breeze has brightened your color so fine;
You stir my mind to write a verse before good wine.
With rain impearled on you, more beautiful you grow;
You're all the more bewitching when about to blow.
The fair forgets to powder her face before you;
The painter hesitates to draw your picture new.
Nor verse nor wine's enough to show delight in me;
I envy butterflies perching deep in your tree.

* *The artist's attitude reveals the beauty of the crabapple flower.*

题菊花

黄　巢

飒飒西风满院栽，
蕊寒香冷蝶难来。
他年我若为青帝，
报与桃花一处开。

To the Chrysanthemum

Huang Chao

In soughing western wind you blossom far and nigh;
Your fragrance is too cold to invite butterfly.
Some day if I as Lord of Spring come into power,
I'd order you to bloom together with peach flower.

* *The poet was the leader of peasant uprising by the end of the Tang Dynasty.*

菊花

黄巢

待到秋来九月八，
我花开后百花杀。
冲天香阵透长安，
满城尽带黄金甲。

The Chrysanthemum

Huang Chao

When autumn comes, the Mountain-climbing Day is nigh;
My flower blows when other blooms come to an end.
In battle array its fragrance rises sky-high,
The capital with its golden armor will blend.

* *The poet speaks as if he were the lord of chrysanthemums in golden armor. The Mountain-climbing Day is the ninth day of the ninth moon according to lunar calendar.*

云

来　鹄

千形万象竟还空，
映水藏山片复重。
无限旱苗枯欲尽，
悠悠闲处作奇峰。

To the Cloud

Lai Hu

You have a thousand shapes in flakes or piles in vain;
Hidden in mountains or on water you remain.
The drought is so severe that all seedlings would die.
Why won't you come down but leisurely tower high?

* *The poet complains that clouds won't turn into rain to combat the drought.*

子　规

吴　融

举国繁华委逝川，
羽毛飘荡一年年。
他山叫处花成血，
旧苑春来草似烟。
雨暗不离浓绿树，
月斜长吊欲明天。
湘江日暮声凄切，
愁杀行人归去船。

To the Cuckoo

Wu Rong

You see your splendor gone with the wind disappear;
You waft with resplendent feather from year to year.
Your tears have dyed the flowers red in alien hill;
But when spring comes to your garden, grass looks green still.
Among the leaves, trees dark in rain long you stay;
At moonset you wail and wait for the dawning day.
On Southern River you sadden the setting sun.
Why should you drown in grief the boat of roaming son?

* *The legend goes that the King of Shu lost his kingdom and turned after his death into a cuckoo which would cry till its tears turned into blood.*

垂柳

唐彦谦

绊惹春风别有情，
世间谁敢斗轻盈？
楚王江畔无端种，
饿损纤腰学不成。

The Weeping Willow

Tang Yanqian

Flirting with vernal breeze, the willow sways so tender.

Who in the world can vie with it but the waist slender?

It is planted at random by the riverside.

How many maids fond of its leaves of hunger died?

* *The poet satirizes the maidens trying to make their waist as slender as willow branch.*

早　梅

齐　己

万木冻欲折，
孤根暖独回。
前村深雪里，
昨夜一枝开。
风递幽香出，
禽窥素艳来。
明年如应律，
先发望春台。

To the Early Mume Blossoms

Qi Ji

Frozen are all the trees;
Your warm root will not freeze.
In the village's deep snow,
Last night your branch did blow.
Fragrance oozed in wind light;
Birds peep at you still white.
If you blossom next year,
You will foretell spring's near.

* *The poet shows he is as pure and cold-proof as the mume blossom.*

焚书坑

章　碣

竹帛烟销帝业虚，
关河空锁祖龙居。
坑灰未冷山东乱，
刘项原来不读书。

The Pit Where Emperor Qin Burned the Classics

Zhang Jie

Smoke of burnt classics gone up with the empire's fall;

Fortresses and rivers could not guard the capital.

Before the pit turned cold, eastern rebellions spread,

The leaders of revolts were not scholars well-read.

* *The poet satirizes the first emperor of the Qin Dynasty who burned up all classics for fear his empire be overthrown without knowing the rebel leaders were not well-read.*

匠心之“美”

李 响

这是一本凝聚了大国工匠智慧和心血的大成之作，许渊冲用英文翻译将国之瑰宝、文之精华带给世界。他的翻译并非传达意思这么简单，常常在完成意思的巧妙转化后又辅以一定的艺术加工：有的一气呵成，有的小心翼翼；有的气吞山河，有的细若游丝。手捧这一本工匠巨制的你和此时的我一样，正穿越古今，横跨中外，享受着一场诗韵的饕餮盛宴！

刚刚接到出版社邀请的时候，我并不平静。“中国翻译文化终身成就奖”，世界文学翻译领域最高奖“北极光”杰出文学翻译奖，中国翻译泰斗……这些在许老身上的光环并不是让我“不平静”的原因。早在意气风发的大学时代，刚刚接触翻译学的我便对“许渊冲”三个字充满了崇敬之情，未曾想过多年后的今天，竟能有幸作为许老经典翻译作品的朗读者，试着用一颗敬畏之心诠释中国传奇的译韵之“美”。于是我经常在戴上耳机面对话筒的时候不断翻阅相关资料，试图参透这位译坛先圣的“音美，形美，意美”。

翻译是个苦差事，“In spring the river rises as high as the sea, and with the river’s tide uprises the moon bright.”（春江潮水连海平，海上明月共潮生）也许是夜明月如钩，许老先生也译思如流，夜不能寐；“Among pine trees bright moonbeams peer; Over crystal stones flows water clear.”（明月松间照，清泉石上流）也许是夜风清月皎，许老反复推敲，最后化繁为简……我的录音室也有一方小小的窗，我也喜欢在晚上工作。我常痴想，抛下白天的繁华，静夜里一盏台灯，一张工作台，一位老者，也是何等的“美”景。说实话，在几百首诗歌的配音朗诵工作中，我丝毫不觉得疲惫，相反，能与读者分享这一片美好的际遇，让人好生流连。

有的翻译是二度创作，有的翻译是忠于原文，这在翻译学中被称作“异化”和“同化”。很显然，许老希望结合两者，并试图将另外一套语言体系中的意蕴之美与原诗结合，不仅仅是还原，更是一种创造。那作为声音演绎者的我呢？我不知道，但我不会掺杂许多个性，许多妄断或者许多修饰，我将怀着一颗崇敬之心，用欣赏的语气尽力保持一个后来者对于先人和先生的情感还原。但有时我也是冲动的，每当录到许老翻译的绝妙之处，我便忘乎所以，由着性子让情感溢出来，填满整个录音室。

这次出版与以往不同，我们尽力完成了“音美”的部分，好诗可吟，许老的翻译强调美感的传达，从来都不是冷冰冰的。就像许老的为人，桀骜、大胆、热情……许老说：“我认为这人生最大的乐趣是创造美，发现美。同样一句话，我翻得比人家好，或者比自己更好，这就是一种乐趣。这个乐趣很大，别人夺不走的。”我希望在配上有声的英文“吟诵”之后，这本书不仅能够更好地传播中国诗歌的含义，更能在听觉上带给读者关于美的享受。

“择一事终一生，不为繁华易匠心。”许老并非繁华中的匠人，他一生经历坎坷，饱经沧桑。100 岁，100 年，一个世纪。2021 年 6 月 17 日下午，我和出版社的编辑约了见面聊许老新书的录音工作，然而却突然得知了许老上午去世的消息。和许老终于未能相见，就让我隔着时空，用声音试着和这位百岁泰斗对话吧。许老曾在一个电视节目里说："这是你们重要的任务之一：使中国文化走向世界，使世界文化更加光辉灿烂！"晚辈一定尽心尽力，不负匠心之"美"，传承大国诗韵。

2021 年 10 月 30 日夜